GREEN
TSUNAMI

A Novella by
Laura Cooney & L.L. Soares

GREEN
TSUNAMI

A Novella by
Laura Cooney & L.L. Soares

Smart Rhino Publications
www.smartrhino.com

First Edition

ISBN-13: 978-0-9896679-4-4
ISBN-10: 0989667944

Dedicated to Jax Bennett,
who left us too soon.

July 28—9:30 a.m.

Joy,

The sky looks like it's on fire.

I know it's not. There's no smoke, no intense heat, no crackling or the smell of things of burning. But there are these wiggly lines in the sky now; flickers might be a better description, and they look like flames. Especially when the sky is red.

It's red a lot of the time.

This is the third time I've written since the shit hit the fan. I'm not really sure what's going on yet. Answers are hard to come by. There's still a green film everywhere, covering all the surfaces, even though the fluid that crashed down on the world has since dried up. I haven't even seen any puddles since it happened.

Things are so different now. It's hard to navigate through this new world without a road map. Nothing is where it should be.

Several times now, I've tried to go outside our neighborhood and get a better idea of how things have changed. Every single time, I have been stopped.

No cars work. Not that I could drive with this one enormous foot of mine. I tried to get behind the steering wheel of a car once since the tsunami, and my foot wouldn't even fit inside the door. And all the cars have transformed, many of them into living creatures that look like cars, but do not have any of the same functions.

Obviously I can't drive a motorcycle or a bicycle. Not that I've tried. But this foot limits me a lot. I assume anything with a motor on it would have undergone the same fate as the cars, anyway. As for bicycles, I see one stranded on the sidewalk once in awhile, but there's no way I could ride it.

I tried walking. Some days I can walk with relative ease, despite my "problem." It's as if the foot is still me and still cooperative. But other days, it throbs so horribly I have no desire to move at all.

I tried to walk downtown to where you are, but whenever I reach the outskirts of the neighborhood, my foot begins to hurt worse than ever. If I try to keep going, it gets so bad I black out. It's like when you use one of those electric collars for dogs. When they reach a certain point, they get shocked. That's what I feel like.

I can't explain it very well.

It seems to cover an eight-block radius. In other words, our neighborhood, more or less. But inside that parameter, I seem to be okay. If you remember, Davey's school is exactly seven blocks away, so I can go there. But if I try to move much further than that, I have to stop.

It's funny how I can get on the Internet sometimes, and how the electricity still works sporadically. But my cell phone won't work at all. I can't get any bars or even a dial tone. Maybe what happened has placed some kind of barrier between the world and the satellites up there. Cell phones work because of satellites, right? And there are towers involved; I know that much. But I'm not sure why my phone won't work. The landlines are dead, too. I'm not sure, doesn't Internet connection work in a similar way? I've never been very knowledgeable in these things.

All I know is, one works and one doesn't.

But it doesn't do me much good if I send out these email messages and you don't respond.

Then again, you probably *can't* respond.

I've emailed everyone in my address book, and *no one* has responded yet. So I'm guessing either they're all dead, or they don't have power, or they just can't be bothered answering emails when they're trying to stay alive.

It's like I'm just talking to myself here.

8

Well, I'm going to shut down now. I don't know how long it will be before I find another place to charge up, and I can't afford to waste energy.

The weather has actually been rather pleasant. Remember the big heat wave just before this happened? It's long gone now. Feels like spring.

Except for the sky. It's such a bright red sometimes. I think my eyes have adjusted to it, but it seems like days go on forever, and the moon forgets to come out.

I hope there's a night tonight. I miss the darkness. It would be a nice break from the redness.

And I hope you get this message.

Love,

Aaron

August 2—2:05 a.m.

Aaron,

I got your messages. I haven't been able to respond until now.

First off, I want to write and tell you I'm alive (no duh, right?). I'm wondering about the look on your face? Are your lips smiling like a juicy earthworm or are they a pinched pink scar? I disappointed you, I know, but I still want that light shining in your eyes for me. I think the bad things I get I deserve. That sounds crazy. I think this dimly lit place with the hot stale air is where I belong. I want you to tell me, "No, Joy. No, you don't belong there."

You used to tell me sweet things until that day when it all changed. I know I'm stupid, but please don't answer, "Yes, Joy, yes, yes, yes. You do deserve this place." I'm sorry. My eyes are blurry with tears. I can't see the damn screen. This email doesn't make sense. Does it? I can't get my thoughts lined up right. It's like I dropped change on the floor and I'm having trouble picking it up.

You sent your emails days ago. I don't even know if you're still alive to read this. But if you are, I want you to smile. Will you do that for me?

I hear them coming. I have to cut off. Write me back. I'll write again when I can.

YELW (your ever-lovin' wife),

Joy

P.S. I'm terrible, I know, but I only just now remembered Davey. How is he?

11

Joy,

You don't know how happy I am to hear from you. I really thought nobody was getting these messages, that I was the only one using email anymore. But I knew, if you were still alive, this would be the way you'd try to contact me.

I really had given up hope.

A few radio stations still work. They're AM stations. I found two that sometimes have actual people talking on them, and one that seems to be on a loop of old news, from before the tsunami. That's all I can get. But I could find out a few things from the live stations. From what I gather, nobody saw this coming. They think about three-quarter of the world's population is dead. It's really hard to tell. I don't know where they come up with those numbers; everything is so chaotic, there's no way to take a census. And where are all the bodies? I've seen a few here and there, but nothing like the numbers I should be seeing.

Supposedly, there are stacks of bodies in certain parts of the country. As if they'd been put aside, away from the remaining survivors. How did that happen?

And those of us who survived have been altered in some way. All different ways, of course. It certainly doesn't lack for variety around here.

You would think that when a big green tsunami pounds down on the earth and floods the streets, and rips buildings out of the ground, that the scientists would have seen something coming. That they could have prepared for it. But this seems to have caught everyone with their pants down.

And it doesn't make sense that anyone survived. Nobody seems to remember when it actually hit. And nobody can figure out how we all didn't get wiped out, how we all didn't just drown.

I've never seen such damage. And at the same time, it all seems to be healing over in some weird way. New things growing in their place—I can't identify most of it. But I'll try if you let me. It would give me something to do if I could catalog this stuff. Name it. You know, like Adam supposedly did when he first became conscious that he was in Eden. He named all the animals and things. That's what I feel like now.

I know. If you were here, you'd say I was an egotist to compare myself to Adam. And you're probably right.

But I'm so eager to tell you about what's happening here that I am totally neglecting your end. Are you still in the office building? Or did you get out? Do you have any clue where you are now?

What's it like there? And when you say "you hear them coming," who are you talking about? It sounds like there are other survivors with you. Would they be angry if they caught you using electricity? You would think they would be happy to get news from the outside world.

Unless you are outside. Just somewhere else. But you mention a dimly lit place. So I assume you're inside somewhere. Maybe you didn't get affected? Maybe you're exactly as I remember you?

Please write back and tell me more.

I'll check again in the morning.

Love you,

Aaron

P.S. I can't talk about Davey yet. I promise I will at some point. But not now.

August 3—4:31 a.m.

Hello Aaron,

This is going to sound terrible, because I should be so happy knowing you're alive and we have a way of talking to each other, but, I got mad after reading your last email. Because I don't know the answers to your questions anymore than you do. The day of the big wave is like the night we drank those pitchers of martinis. I know some evil shit happened and I was right there watching, but it's all shadows to me.

I remember being at my desk that morning. And one of the cheap-ass pens they have here leaked ink onto my new skirt (white linen of course!) and, it seemed like the worst thing that could happen. I shouted "Fuck off!" loud enough so that Cindy, the office prude, shot me a dirty look (she was the moron who went to HR to complain about my blouse being low-cut … well, I guess she knows now there are worst things than that, LOL).

I was on my way to the bathroom to blot the stain when that ass, Bradley Bascom, stopped me and told me to come listen to his radio. I was gonna tell him what he could do with Rush Limbaugh's latest gas blast, until I saw how scared he looked. I didn't even ask what it was about because I knew it was something very bad and I wanted to put off hearing it for as long as possible.

We walked fast over to his desk. People were standing listening with white faces, looking like there was a mosquito buzzing around their heads they couldn't get rid of. I got this sick feeling in my stomach before I even heard the newscaster.

"But we don't get tsunamis here," I remember saying.

15

"Maybe it's the Rapture," Cindy said.

Nobody replied to that. The floor started shaking like there was an earthquake, and then a fluorescent green light blinded me for a second. After that is when my recollection gets shadowy. I have these disjointed images of people running down the stairwell. Someone falling, getting trampled and screams. I remember feeling wet at some point, like I was underwater, but it didn't last very long.

I think we wound up underground somewhere. I don't know where or how. I think they keep the lights down low on purpose so we can't see them so well. Because we might recognize them. They have heads like the balloons in Macy's Parade. We even call them "Balloon Heads." Do they have them where you are? I feel like I know who they are, but they can't be regular people. They must be aliens or something?

When I got your first email, I didn't answer it right away, because even though I could read it okay, it was like I forgot how to write. I couldn't put the words from my head onto the screen. Then, when I could, I felt so confused. I felt like I was putting a bunch of letters together that didn't spell anything and you wouldn't understand what I was telling you. But now my mind's clearing and it's getting easier. I'm telling you it's like the worst hangover ever. Not just with the throbbing head and the fog in my brain, but the throwing up until all that was left was bile.

There are people I know here. Bradley and Cindy (why couldn't it be people I like?) and others I never saw before and the Balloon Heads. It seems like I should know them somehow.

That's all I can tell you for now. I have to go. We've got chores and shit we have to do.

YFHW (your foggy-headed wife),

Joy

P.S. How come you can't tell me about Davey? I had to force myself to ask that. I don't think I want to know.

16

August 3—10:06 a.m.

I'm shocked they had enough time to say anything on the radio. It all happened so suddenly. And it came out of nowhere. I know that no one had said a word about it before it happened. If the scientists saw it coming, they didn't say a word. For some reason, I think they were just as surprised as we were.

I wasn't sure if you knew about this already, but most of the people who were touched by that green water … it changed us all in some way. I think I mentioned that last time. I was in the backyard when it happened, working on the garden. Pulling out weeds around the strawberry plants. One minute everything was completely normal, and the next I felt like I was inside a blender. It was all so strange and disorienting. I tried to save some things from the house, but the wood had all turned into some kind of sludge, and it was collapsing in on itself. Luckily I hadn't been in there, or I might have been buried alive in that muck.

But I am different. Not too much, as far as I can tell. But one of my feet is gigantic now. I told you that already, right? It's swollen up to the size of a medium-sized dog. It looks really strange, and it makes it hard to move around, but I manage. Sometimes, I have to drag it along behind me when I walk. Other times I'm able to walk just fine with it, like it was the most natural thing in the world. It's like sometimes it's numb and useless, and other times it has complete sensation and I can move on it without even thinking. Either way, I've learned how to deal with it. I've adjusted.

I've seen a couple of the ones with the big heads. They look helpless. Or at least the ones I saw did. Their heads are so big, they can't lift them. They can't move. I felt horrible for them. But there was

17

something weird about them, too. Something that made me *feel* weird. That made me want to get away from them. Get as far away as I could.

What kind of chores do they make you do? They haven't hurt you at all, have they?

Davey was at school when it happened.

I haven't seen him in days.

So much for being Mister Mom. I couldn't even keep the house from falling apart.

Look, I know we weren't in a good place that day. We'd been mad at each other for a while, and we weren't getting along. We even discussed a separation. I don't know if you remember that. But that's all behind us, now. Everything's changed. I'm not mad anymore. Hell, I don't even know what we were mad about.

I'm just glad you're alive.

But I wish I knew where you were. And I wish I could get there, and take you away. We could start over again.

My foot is throbbing. The big one. It gets pretty painful sometimes. I think I'm going to sign off now. I'll try to write again soon.

Aaron

August 3—8:05 p.m.

Hi Aaron,

It is funny you would feel bad for the Balloon Heads. Did you miss the part where I told you they are holding me captive? That I and the others stranded here with me are their virtual slaves? I don't know why you are always siding with others, against me, even complete strangers. Even strange alien creatures, who for all we know are the ones who caused all this chaos and destruction in the first place. How am I supposed to allow you to forgive me when you act like this?

Since you let our house get destroyed, where do you live? I envy you because I haven't seen the sun or breathed fresh air since this catastrophe. I wonder why you didn't put the garden hose on the house and stop it from melting? The Balloon Heads do not seem able to speak, but somehow they are able to access our thoughts to indicate what they want us to do. They told us the atmosphere outside is polluted and we would die if we were to leave the hive, as they call this place. I am woken up at odd hours of the very early morning and led to this room full of computers, not by any being, but by something in my head that tells me where to go. So, hard as it is to believe, I think the Balloon Heads want me to communicate with you, but for what purpose?

I want to write to you. I want to know how you are, what you are doing, and what you are thinking. If a Balloon Head is reading this, I want them to know that I do not care and we will continue to write regardless. We are not afraid, nor will we be manipulated into feeling despair or panic.

Our chores are the chores of home health care aid. The Balloon Heads have powerful minds, but they are physically helpless. We must feed them and bathe them. Bring them to the toilet and wipe their butts for them. Massage their limbs so their muscles do not atrophy. Why do we do it? I do not understand it myself. It is a compulsion they put into our minds that we must perform every day, over and over.

Will this pollution of mind spread to the outside through our emails? Through the emails that everyone who lives within the hive sends out to loved ones? I wonder how many get answers. No one is telling.

But it's the perfect mode of transmission. Are we going to stop our only method of contact? You tell me, Aaron. Is hearing from me worth the risk? Should I tell you in my noblest sounding voice: "Stay away from me. My words are an infectious disease. Keep me in your heart, but remove me from your contact list?"

I don't want to stop. I can't stop. You are the only one who can stop this. If I don't hear from you again, I will know that your fear is more powerful than your love.

WFAT (with fear and trepidation),

Joy

P.S. You must never let Davey read these emails.

August 4—8:48 a.m.

I didn't say that I sympathized with the Balloon Heads that were holding you captive. You always twist my words around. Nice to know some things haven't changed.

 I don't know anything about them, and I certainly wouldn't side with them. I was talking about some I saw here, on the outside. The ones here certainly aren't enslaving anyone, and they are probably just going to die of starvation unless someone takes pity on them. But nobody has yet. Not that there are many of us. I might see someone every three or four days, and it's not for long. But everyone avoids the Balloon Heads. They can sense something wrong about them.

I guess the ones here are weak, and there aren't enough of them to cause any trouble.

But they don't look like aliens. They look like us. Except they have enormous heads. Like my foot. I think they're just changed people.

I wish I knew more about what happened to you.

The news says the tsunami changed the atmosphere somehow. That it's different now, and we've been changed to survive in it. So that does seem to make sense with what they told you. That the outside might be poisonous to you if you aren't changed. But at the same time, I don't know what to believe. If the Balloon Heads are transformed, which they obviously are, then they have to breathe the altered air. If they survive in the same space you do, then you must be able to breathe it, too.

Does that make sense?

I'll find you. Somehow.

23

Every day I try to walk out to that invisible barrier I mentioned. And every day it gets so painful I can't go on. But I'm trying. I'm trying real hard to get to you.

Love,

Aaron

August 4—10:27 a.m.

Joy,

You know how they say the cockroaches will outlast us all? I guess they were right. I was standing next to this big puddle this morning, the first water I've seen in days that wasn't in bottles. Almost a small lake, really. And suddenly, it started to move. The sun was reflecting off it, and I realized it was thousands of cockroaches with mirrored wings. They looked almost like jewels as they scurried away. Or made of glass. They'd been transformed too, but they were still around.

I should have expected as much.

But I have to admit, they were actually beautiful. Nothing like the filthy little buggers that used to creep me out when we went to visit your mother in the Bronx. Remember how she used to put down poison and roach traps and that Chinese chalk stuff. They'd go away awhile, but they always came back. I remember one time I was at one of my first jobs, when we first got married, and all of these women were screaming about something in the break room. I went over and lifted some papers and there was the biggest roach I had ever seen. I swear it was bigger than my hand. So big and bloated that it could barely move. It was completely harmless, the way it was all bloated up like that, but for some reason it really touched something inside me, something repellent, and I almost wanted to scream, too. It was just so hideous. That was the last time I ever laughed at someone for screaming about bugs or mice or something. It was just horrible. I still have nightmares about that thing.

I have no idea where the roaches scattered to. I mean, they were pretty and reflecting and all, and then they were gone. I didn't see them enter

27

any holes in the ground or anything. And I haven't seen them since. They sure are good at hiding.

Are there any roaches in the building where you're living?

I remember the times I visited you at your job, bringing Davey to visit you during your lunch break when you first went back to work. Remember that? I thought it looked like a nice enough building. Modern-looking. Not too old. All that glass and steel. I wonder what it looks like now.

Aaron

August 4—7:11 p.m.

Aaron,

Per usual, you ignore what I tell you. Do you think what I told you about the Balloon Heads controlling my thoughts and possibly using my emails to infiltrate yours is a part of what you so lovingly refer to as my "craziness?"

I remember you used to pretend not to hear certain things I said. Things that you considered paranoid or delusional. Aaron, why do you always end up making me hate you? How come you didn't say you were sorry I had to clean up the Balloon Heads' shit? All I get from you is some crap about cockroaches. I wish I was a cockroach so I could scurry away and hide in the walls.

What can I tell you about the building? It's just fucking dark. Didn't I tell you that? At night, I grind my teeth. The only way I know whether it's morning or night is by looking at the time display at the bottom of this laptop. Who knows if that's even accurate or not? I get so angry at times my chest starts shaking.

Cindy and I had to bathe this Balloon Head today we call Woody. The Balloon Heads don't speak so they can't tell us their names, but we call him Woody because he is always having erections. At first, I was horribly embarrassed by it, now I think it's funny. It seemed to come to Cindy and I at the same time that we were to give this pervert a bath. I know because the moment the command to bathe him was put into my head, I looked at Cindy and she was staring back at me with this horrified look on her face. How do you explain that? Hmm?

I don't know about the outside world, but in here, the Balloon Heads sit in wheelchairs all day long and stare at the floor. I got up and starting pushing Woody's wheelchair to the bathroom. Cindy followed, dragging her feet. All the Balloon Heads wear these fugly pink polyester jogging suits. Cindy took off Woody's top so I'd have to deal with his bottoms (she's such a fucking prude). They don't wear underwear, so as soon as I pulled down his elastic waistband there it was … boing! Bad enough I have to look at one swollen head.

Cindy closed her eyes as we lifted him into the tub. That sucker was heavy. I think I pulled a muscle in my back. Then, when we're soaping him down, trying to ignore the elephant (snake?) in the room, the thought penetrates us that there's another use for all that soapy lather on our hands. Cindy looks at me as if to say, "*You* do it."

"I'm a married woman," I tell her straight out.

Cindy pouts and says, "I'm a virgin." (And yet I remember hearing about how she came out of the VP of Marketing's office one day with flushed face, bed head, lipstick smeared, and her shirt buttoned up crooked.)

"This will be good practice then," I said.

Then the compulsion overtakes us and we're both lathering his pole. Cindy starts crying.

"Shut up and jerk," I tell her.

I gotta admit, I cracked myself up, especially seeing the look on her face after I said it. I couldn't stop laughing. Cindy was bawling and I was cackling and Woody the Balloon Head was erupting like a snow-peaked Vesuvius.

Maybe you think I'm making this shit up to get a reaction out of you? Think what you want. You always do anyway. I'm exhausted and my back is killing me. I'm going to bed.

LMBHJ (Little Miss Balloon Head Jerker-offer),

Joy

P.S. Probably not a good idea relaying this story to Davey?

30

August 4—10:45 p.m.

Joy,

That was a pretty horrible story about the Balloon Heads. I'm really sorry that they're putting you through all that. Now I really want to find you and take you away from there.

I met some other survivors tonight. It's rare when they want to interact. Everyone pretty much just keeps to themselves these days. But there are three of them. Two men and a woman. At first, I thought they were going to try to rob me, but there's really nothing they could take. And they assured me it was all a misunderstanding. I guess I'm just jumpy, after all that's happened. And it's not like I get many chances to use my social skills anymore. The situation got better after that. We all realized we're in the same boat, and it just wouldn't help anything to prey on one another.

I'm guessing they were teenagers before everything happened, or at least in their early twenties, and they've clearly known each other for a long time. They have all these inside jokes and keep smiling at one another.

Thomas, the older one, has these really big teeth that stick out of his mouth all the time. And buggy eyes. His nose is pretty long and twisted, like a tree branch. He always seems very nervous.

The woman's name is Katie. I guess she's more like a girl. I would be surprised if she wasn't a freshman in college or something. She wears this wrinkled school uniform and has long, dirt-encrusted hair. You can tell she used to be cute. But now half her face won't move, and she has one really large hand that she drags on the ground behind her. The other guy is named Chet and he's got a beard and his eyes are so big

31

they protrude from his head, just like a frog. And they're always leaking green fluid.

They're probably got other imperfections I can't see.

I'm in one of the other houses in our neighborhood now. Not all of them changed or collapsed. I've been in this one before. It's good because the electricity works. I think the three of them are out sleeping in the garage.

They said we should stay together, but I don't know. I'm not much of a joiner, and I have been getting along just fine by myself. It's nice to have other people around, but there's still something about them I don't trust, and I doubt I'll go with them when they move on.

I saw the roaches again. There was a Balloon Head in the middle of the street that had died, and this swarm of the mirrored roaches covered him. A few minutes later, they crawled off, and big sections of his body had been eaten down to the bone. They didn't touch his head, though, just stripped the flesh off his body. I sure hope they only eat dead things.

And they disappeared as quickly as they'd come.

I might leave before morning comes. I know a place where I can go, where they won't find me. And then they'll just move on. I'm really thinking I'd prefer to stay behind. Let them go on without me.

There was some canned food in the cupboards, but nothing that I recognized. The labels were all in some language I couldn't read, and the pictures on the cans were just bizarre. We opened some of them. We had to eat something. But they tasted strange. One can had these squirmy white fungi in them—like big, slimy mushroom caps. I don't feel so well now. I hope it wasn't the food.

What do they feed you where you are? Is it anything like the old cafeteria food they used to serve there before the tsunami, or has that changed, too?

Aaron

August 5—3:00 a.m.

Aaron, Aaron, Aaron. You poor naïve bastard. You would trust deformed, homeless thieves? There is no one you can trust in this world. NO ONE.

I wish I could get away from people. Not just the Balloon Heads (do they even count as people?), but everyone, including Cindy and Bradley. At first, when we were new to this dark, hot Purgatory, we were, most of us, like helpless mewling kittens looking to be petted and fed.

It's like everyone here is from an office building or maybe just my office building. People from other companies who were on other floors and cleaning people. I recognize a few of the Spanish people here, dressed in their orange cleaning smocks. I was thinking a bit ago how, when things were normal, we never said, 'hello' to them as we passed them in the hall, as they removed the dirty bags from our wastebaskets and put clean bags in, as they wheeled their cleaning carts around bathrooms. It's like they existed on a lower level from us. We tsk, tsk at the caste system in India. Untouchables and all that. We like to pretend we don't have a caste system in this country. Americans love to pat themselves on the back, don't they?

I remember Cindy one time left a ring on the sink in the bathroom and when she went back to get it, it was gone and she told me, "It must have been that cleaning girl."

"How do you know?" I asked.

"That's how they get by in their country," Cindy said, "They steal."

"Is that a fact?" I asked.

"Minimum wage isn't good enough for them. They think they deserve more, so they steal our stuff."

"You try paying rent, food, electricity, supporting a family on minimum wage," I said.

"They can't even speak English," Cindy said. "You think I'd get a job in their country not speaking Spanish?"

And now we're on the same level as "them." There's always a "them," isn't there? The Balloon Heads are the new "them." And we are their 'them." I wonder if they look down on us like we did on the Mexicans.

Funniest of all is that Cindy has been walking all bug-eyed and ticked out since we gave Woody that bath. And this little Mexican dude who used to empty the trash cans around here gave Cindy this tiny toy burro that looked like a child had knitted it (maybe his daughter?). The stitching was all crooked and the black buttons that were sewn on for eyes didn't even match. But Cindy had this quivering smile on her lips when she took it from him and he (his name is Jose, I found out from Cindy of all people) petted Cindy on the head like she was a little girl. Maybe he was thinking of his daughter? I'm sure he misses her. I wish I could say I missed Davey, but I don't feel like I do.

Maybe he left his daughter behind. I wonder if everything is as weird there as it is here.

I know what the "right things" are, but I don't feel them. I should probably stop judging Cindy so much. Seems like she made a connection. I didn't. But at least I just figured out by writing to you that we are the new Mexicans. And the Balloon Heads are the new "us." Does that make sense? Probably not.

UNT (until next time),

Joy (maybe I should rename myself Juana, lol!)

August 6—3:22 a.m.

Joy,

After I wrote to you last night, I went out to the living room in the house and found them at it. Kind of grotesque. Their nudity just emphasized the ways their bodies had been deformed. There were tumors I hadn't noticed before, and their strange version of sex involved lots of licking and the fondling of oversized body parts. It ended with a bizarre game of Twister, where the two men twisted their bodies to avoid bulges and growths, to penetrate the woman at the same time. Her vaginal lips were as huge as their penises were malformed. I can honestly say there was very little about the spectacle that I would consider arousing. It was more of a curiosity than anything else. I watched for a little while, then went back to my hiding space.

They searched around for me a little this morning, but gave up pretty easily. I'm staying hidden for the rest of the day, just in case. I have no idea if they are trustworthy or not, but I'm not willing to take the chance. On one hand, it would be really nice to have friends at this point. Everything is so disjointed and chaotic. On the other hand, my instincts said these three were a little off from the first time I saw them, and I'm thinking it might be a good idea to listen to my instincts right now.

That's interesting about your theory about the class system stuff. Sounds like everything is pretty twisted right now. It's been awhile since I worked in an office, but I know exactly what you're talking about.

It sounds like you have a decent amount of time to yourself, though. You're not serving those Balloon Head things constantly at least. How

37

much time do they give you to yourself? It sounds like you've still got some semblance of your life going on.

I have to admit, I feel adrift in these new surroundings. I've been trying to keep on the move, mostly because I'm not sure what's safe anymore and I don't want to stay in one place for too long. But it's tough when you're limited to one area. I'm really surprised I haven't seen more people.

I'm thinking of going to see Davey soon. He's still at the school, and I've only seen him once since the tsunami hit. I don't think I really want to see him again, but there's some unfinished business I should take care of. And I want to see how much more he's changed.

I know he was a major headache growing up, always getting into trouble. And I know it really freaked you out that time you caught him torturing that cat. That bothered me a lot, too. You know what they say about serial killers starting out small as kids, hurting animals. I think that scared the shit out of us. And I still believe he's a big reason why we drifted apart. I know toward the end you just wanted nothing to do with him, and I can understand that. I don't know if he's sociopathic or what. But if he continued to get worse, we probably would have had to commit him somewhere. His behavior just kept getting worse and worse. I just couldn't handle him at the end, and it was just getting out of control.

Did I tell you that he pulled a knife on me once? I was asking him questions and he got agitated and pulled out this knife. It wasn't huge or anything, but it was the action that freaked me out. That he would pull a knife on his own father.

Yeah, I still think Davey played a big part in what happened to us.

It's funny, the day before the tsunami, his principal called me into the office to discuss his behavior. He was starting to get violent with the other kids. The principal, that Mr. Atkins guys, he told me if things didn't change soon, they'd have to ask Davey to leave. Well, that's all water under the bridge now. (No pun intended.) I don't even know if Atkins survived. The school was probably taken over by the children for all I know.

38

I went to pick him up after the tsunami ended. After things stopped rattling apart around us. I went to the school and stood there in the demolished parking lot. The cars all overgrown with slime and weird plant life. Davey's face was in one of the windows, and I waved to him. But he was different. His features were bloated and distorted. He stared at me, but didn't respond. That's the last time I saw him. I saw some other kids staring out, too, but none of them had the intense glare Davey had. The others all seemed to be staring vacantly, but it was clear Davey was aware of everything. Especially me, standing there, looking at him.

I felt so uncomfortable, I couldn't bring myself to go inside and get him, and my foot started hurting, so I just left. But I know I have to face my responsibility to him. I have to at least go and talk to him. He is our son, after all. Our flesh and blood.

But I'm afraid he's become worse than ever now.

I just keep thinking of that knife he pulled, and I wonder how safe it is to go back there, and try to talk to him. But I've got to get some closure.

The school is right where it used to be. It's changed, though. It almost looks like a living thing now, with windows that almost look like glassy eyes, and some of it has tunneled underground. I'm betting your building is similar.

I wonder if Davey will try to kill me this time.

Aaron

August 6—9:15 a.m.

Aaron,

For some reason, I felt compelled to write to you later than usual this morning. I found myself wondering if there was a reason. If today was something special.

It occurred to me, looking at the date on your last email: August 6th. That was the date we bombed Hiroshima. Why do I remember that date? I don't know. Why do I say "we" dropped the A-bomb? We weren't even alive in 1945. It's the collective "we" of community. Somehow we are all complicit in it, as we are in the green tsunami. Don't take this to mean I have any inside knowledge about the tsunami. I don't. If the Balloon Heads know anything, they aren't talking, not even telepathically.

So why this weird guilt? I remember when I first wrote you, I said I felt like I deserved to suffer the effects of the tsunami. I think it goes beyond that. I feel like all of us deserve it. I couldn't say that to anyone but you. Imagine if I spoke that thought out loud here? Everyone would pounce on me in hatred and condemnation.

When you wrote that Davey had changed, I felt a gloating pleasure. You think I turned away from you and Davey because I was disgusted and scared of him? The truth is that I was afraid I was responsible for his behaving the way he did. I have thoughts about wanting to hurt people. Not physically, but with words and behavior. Sometimes I say things just for the sake of upsetting people. I think, as a baby, Davey sensed this. Cruelty bonded him to me. I saw your kindness as a weakness until I saw how unkind Davey was. Then I realized the weakness was in me, and that was what made me turn away from you.

41

So, yes, I deserve every humiliation the Balloon Heads put upon me and every bit of the mindless drudgery. But drudgery's too boring. I'd rather have more explicit punishment. So jerking off Woody didn't upset me so much. I was thinking along the lines of, "Abuse. Now you're talking." Cindy mistook that for strength. She said to me, "How do you go on, Joy? Like this is one long, normal day of work?"

I got smart and told her, "It's the same as before except our bosses are the Balloon Heads now."

I suppose in a way that is true. Or maybe I'm just a twisted fuck. Just like the fruit of our loins is. I guess little Davey is what you'd call a bad apple? Yes, I know. Me and my bad jokes. I still make bad jokes even here. People like my jokes even less than they used to. I guess when you're a slave, the first thing that goes is your sense of humor.

KOLTTT (keep on laughing through the tears),

Joy

August 7—2:31 p.m.

Joy,

As I write this, I can hear Davey calling my name, and it is the most horrifying thing I have ever heard.

I'm in what once was the principal's office, I'm guessing. Although it's a lot different now. The walls are covered in scales and seem to be breathing. But the computer works, and I'm able to write, so there's no time like the present. Might as well tell you the whole story while it's fresh in my mind.

I really hesitated coming into the building, but I convinced myself that, even if I move on without him, I had to talk to Davey face-to-face one more time. No matter what his behavior was, or what he has become, he's still our son. And I owe him at least a good-bye.

But things here were along the lines of what I thought they would be. Even worse.

Whatever adults ran this place are long gone. I didn't see any sign of teachers or administrators. But there are lots of children. So many, I was shocked to find so many had survived. Their parents are probably all dead. But they're not even really children anymore. They've just become these bulbous, crab-footed things that scurry across the floor and babble nonsense to themselves. I swear, when I first saw one of them, it scared the hell out of me. They're not quite human, and yet, looking into their scared little eyes, they're the most human creatures you could ever see. Their hands are transformed into claws, and they can't turn doorknobs, so it's easy enough to trap them inside rooms by simply closing the doors. But then they begin to cry—they sound like mewling kittens—and it's heartbreaking to hear their sounds.

I saw Davey.

He was in the room that at one time had to be the school gymnasium. He's gigantic now. Like some great, glowing caterpillar who runs the length of the once-polished wood floors. It is difficult for him to move, and his arms are short and useless now, like a Tyrannosaurus Rex. His body seems to have sucked many of the other children into him. That's the only way I can describe it. Occasionally, their faces pop up to the surface of his vast hide. But above all the mutated flesh is the oversized head of our Davey. He's not quite a Balloon Head, as you call them, but every part of him is so overgrown that he looks an awful lot like one of those huge floats they used to have in the Macy's Thanksgiving Day parades. Imagine a living, breathing float, and you'll have an idea of what Davey has become.

It's so strange to see him this way, because he was always such a thin boy.

Any questions I had about whether Davey was truly in charge of his hideous mass were put to rest when I entered the room. His eyes immediately darted toward me, and he tried to move his undulating body toward me. Unsuccessfully, I might add. He is large, but very awkward. It's clear he has little control of his own body anymore.

"Father!" he shouted upon seeing me. "You've finally come to take me home."

But we both knew this was some sick joke. There was no way I was taking him anywhere like he was now. And he knew that.

"Hello, Davey," I said. Not sure what else I was going to say to him, even as I stood before him.

"You left me here," he said. "I saw you outside, waiting for me, the day after it happened. You had come for me. But you refused to come inside. You ran away at the sight of me."

"A lot has happened," I said to him. "Everything is different now."

"Even a father's love for his child?" Davey asked. He always did know how to push my buttons. Even when I concluded long ago that I did not like this child I'd helped bring into the world, that

never overshadowed the guilt I felt. The pain of not being able to love my own son, no matter how hard I tried.

It made sense that he would absorb other children into his being. He had always been a bully, and instead of emotional intimidation, his *flesh* now intimidated them, devouring them whole. In some strange way, it seemed like the logical progression.

Like I said, as he stood there, the faces of other children came forward, pressing against his flesh like glass, peering out at me. In various voices, I heard them call "Daddy?" and "Mommy?" in these sad little voices, and then retreat beneath the surface of his skin when they realized their mistake.

"So, what made you come back now?" Davey asked. "After all this time?"

"I had to see you, one last time," I said. "I had to at least try to save you. But it's clear you don't need saving from this place. You're in charge here now."

"Am I, father?" he asked. He spoke so strangely. He was always a smart kid, despite his problems. But the way he talked was so clinical, and like a monotone. Devoid of any emotions. "My movements are limited. And I am a prisoner here. Any nourishment I get comes from the other children, and they are getting scarce. It's true there are no predators here that can harm me. I am the summit of the food chain. But that is poor consolation indeed."

As I stood before him, something in his eyes told me he was resigned to his fate. He knew that he would die in this place, probably of starvation once his prey was exhausted. He did not fool himself. He knew I was not there to save him.

"I'm sorry, Davey," I told him. "I'm sorry I wasn't a better father to you. I'm sorry that I can't help what you have become."

"Don't worry," he told me. "It's been a long time since I cared enough to resent you or my mother for your treatment of me. You were simply caretakers, bringing me into the world. But your roles are meaningless to me now. You are not a part of this new ecosystem I live in. You are not a part of my world anymore. So such things as regrets just don't matter anymore."

"I wanted to say I was sorry, anyway," I told him.

"Apology accepted," he said, though I could see the malice in his eyes. Despite his protest, I knew that he still had strong feelings toward me. Feelings of hatred he could not conceal.

Part of his vast serpentine body revealed large, pit-like pores that opened and closed as he breathed. More faces pushed close to the surface to watch me, and then fell back into his body. Davey had become a truly ferocious creature indeed.

He kept trying to move closer to me. To absorb me too, no doubt. But I stayed just far enough away.

There was a sweet smell that filled the room. It reminded me of cherries. He probably used this scent to attract the crab-like children who remained free of him.

"So this is the end of our relationship," he said, and I could sense the slightest sadness in his voice. "There is nowhere for things to go from here."

"Yes," I said. "I believe that's true."

"Then you are of no use to me," he said. "Please go away. I can't stand to look at you anymore."

He didn't have to tell me a second time. I left that room, trying hard not to break into a run. Of course, with this swollen foot of mine, it's impossible to run. But I wish I could have. I dragged my bad foot all the way to the office I am in now.

I must leave soon. The breathing walls seem to be closing in, inch by inch, and I'm afraid if I stay here, they will smother me.

On the way out, I'll open the doors to the rooms I trapped them in, and let the crab-like children out. They are the last remaining ones that Davey has not devoured, and I know that eventually they will go to him and accept their fate. I pity them, and yet I could not bring myself to keep Davey from getting them. Besides, what would they do in a locked room but waste away and die? Better that they could provide Davey with a bit more sustenance.

It was my final gift to him.

Does that sound heartless?

I've got to sign off now. I'll try to write again soon, when I am far away from this place.

Aaron

August 8—3:18 a.m.

Querida Aaron,

Me miran. Estoy aprendiendo espanol. That means: Look at me. I'm learning Spanish. Jose is trying to teach me and Cindy. I'm not very good at it, but it keeps my mind off things. A Thing. *Cosa* in Spanish. A *monstruo.* *Monstruo* is another word for Davey. If Davey lived here among us Mexicans.

Forgive my facetiousness regarding our son. If I didn't make a little joke out of it, my soul would bleed orange on the floor. That's why I didn't write you for two days. My insides turned orange. Don't ask me how I know this, but I'm sure of it. That color scares me. Davey's skin had an orange tinge. Did you ever notice? Of course, that's nothing compared to the way you've described how he looks now.

Davey is smart. Why does someone who is smart choose to be evil? I have a sick feeling in my stomach. I think the Balloon Heads know about Davey.

You know how Bradley was always a brown-noser? Well, that hasn't changed. He does more than we're compelled to do for the Balloon Heads. He was the one who first recognized the Balloon Head we call Tomato (because of his plump, red face). Even in the dimness, we could make out the redness in his face. That's how flushed he is.

Bradley was being extremely attentive to Tomato, giving him foot massages, cutting his toenails, putting a pillow under his neck. I asked him what he was up to.

Bradley looked at me smugly and said, "Don't recognize him, do you, honey?"

49

"Some say he's Tomato. Others say he's *To-matto*," I said. (I have no idea how to write that phonetically, but you know the old phrase.)

"That's Rafe Dinkle," Bradley told me. "VP of Marketing."

"I know who Rafe Dinkle is, you turd," I said. "But last time I checked, he didn't have hydrocephalus."

"And we're not in Kansas anymore, are we? Take a look at his right hand."

Dinkle had a scar on his right hand that looked like a half swastika. We used joke about it. "Der Fuhrer will see you now," and like that. And that damn Tomato has the exact same scar. Remember me telling you how the Balloon Heads seemed familiar? Every damn last one of them is an executive. You believe that shit? Even when it's the end of the fucking world, they still come out on top. Top-heavy, but top nevertheless.

The lighting is lousy here, but I'm squinting at the Balloon Heads, noticing bulbous noses, pointed chins, caterpillar eyebrows, and other identifying features of our executive class. Is that how you were able to recognize Davey?

After I read your email about Davey, Bradley asked me out of the blue, a few hours later, "How is your son?"

He's not exactly what you'd call a solicitous person. Well, not unless you're in a position of power or can benefit him in some way. He's never asked me about family or weekend plans or anything like that. So it seemed odd. I think the Balloon Heads put it in his mind to ask. I considered not emailing you after Bradley asked about Davey.

These emails are dangerous. Didn't I tell you? I'd like to write more about my situation, but I'm afraid to. I don't know if they'd allow that?

YOW (your orange wife),

Joy

August 8—8:40 p.m.

Joy,

Am I relieved to hear from you. After no word for two days, I was starting to worry that something bad had happened on your end. I'm glad that you're alive.

I know you're concerned about the Balloon Heads listening in on our conversations over the Internet (I guess *listening* isn't the right word), but I swear I'd rather hear from you and risk it than not hear from you and think we're safe. Besides, if those things can read your mind, then nothing is safe anyway. So why not keep me abreast of the situation on your end?

Soon after my last email, I ran out of that pulsating organism that had once been Davey's school. It was getting hard to stay there. The cloying smells, the breathing walls. I just couldn't stand it anymore.

As I ran down the hallway (well, as much of a run as I can do), to the exit door, I could still hear Davey calling my name, begging me to come back. He said he wanted to talk more with me. That he wanted me to hold him like I did when he was little. But I know his true intention. He was hungry and wanted to devour me like he did the others.

I wonder if the teachers were inside him as well, or if they got away somehow. The faces that kept surging forth from him, none of them appeared to be adults. But I can't be certain.

He was such a grotesque vision. I know he will continue to haunt my dreams.

I am never going back there. I said what I could. There's no point in returning.

I guess it makes sense that your Balloon Heads were once the bosses. I'm not sure why that mutation would be so selective as to infect only people in authority, but somehow it doesn't surprise me.

Have you had a chance to explore your surroundings at all? Or do they only keep you in that one part of the building, to provide care to those creatures and then return to your cubical? If you're able to get away and see more of the building—how it has transformed—let me know what you find. I'm curious to hear what kinds of metamorphoses have happened on your end.

Are you sure that nothing about you has changed. No enlarged extremities? No other abnormalities? I was so happy when you told me you had not changed. But seriously, if you're different, no matter what the change, please do not hesitate to tell me. You know I will understand.

I'm back in the park now. There are birds I've never seen before. Some kind of peacocks. Their necks trail into stinging tendrils instead of a head and beak, and their feathers are so radiant and colorful, they are mesmerizing. I saw one catch a rodent that got too close, and the tendrils wrapped around it and pulled it into a maw that suddenly opened up in its neck.

Luckily, they seem to be scared of humans.

The creatures on this earth now are simply amazing to behold. So much beauty and so much cruelty.

I killed one of the birds with stones. A big rock took it off balance. A few more brought it down. I cut away the weird tendrils and sliced up its meat and cooked it over an open flame. The meat was blue! And yet it tasted so much like duck. Remember how much you used to love duck? You'd always order it when we went out to eat.

The weather is getting warmer. I saw a few more humans today. But they kept their distance. Nobody trusts anyone else. Soon, they were gone.

52

I am getting tired of being alone. If I wasn't so sane, I might go back to Davey's school, just to have someone to talk to.

Please don't stop writing.

Aaron

August 9—2:52 a.m.

Aaron,

I am envious of the light in your world and all the beautiful things it allows you to see. Living in darkness changes you. The dark feels like a presence, like a solid, solemn thing that makes you speak in whispers. It's always there, covering you. Sometimes I like that feeling of being hidden. You can make faces at people or flip them the bird without them knowing.

But it drives me crazy not knowing what is in the shadows. There is enough light to see, but only faintly. How do I know what I'm actually eating? You said your bird meat was blue. I have no idea of what colors I am eating. Remember that childhood game where you close your eyes and someone puts an object in your hand and you have to guess what it is? I got it wrong so many times.

I examine things by the light of the computer screen. I don't see any changes in my body but there are no mirrors here. I look into the black of the screen to see the reflection of my face. I don't notice any difference. Some of the women cry about not having make-up, but what is the point of wearing make-up in the dark?

I run my fingers over everything like I'm Helen Keller. I thought it was my newly enhanced sense of touch that made the walls and floor feel like they were alive, but after what you've told me about the breathing walls, I'm beginning to think there is a life force inhabiting them. The walls feel as soft and fuzzy as a young girl's skin. The floor is warm at times and cool at others. Yet the room temperature never seems to change.

I've heard burps and farts that seem to emanate from the air. We usually end up blaming them on Bradley, LOL. Did I ever tell you the Balloon Heads make a sound that sounds like a cricket but throatier? That's the only noise they ever make. I wish Richard Widmark was here to throw them down the stairs in their wheelchairs. Their bodies are like the bodies of ventriloquist dummies. The huge heads are the only part of them that seems alive.

I like how my white skin seems to glow in the darkness, but I can't help but think they are keeping it dark to hide some terrible secret. My eyes are getting good at making out things in shadows. It sounds silly, but sometimes, I imagine I'm a cat, hunting in the night. Unfortunately, I'm not a good "mouser."

Sounds are haunting when you can't see where they're coming from. I imagine that all the words spoken here echo, but they don't. I know they don't, but the darkness makes it seem like they do.

If I stepped out of this place and went back into your world, Aaron, I'd be "blinded by the light" like they sang in that old song. I think that was Manfred Mann's Earth Band? Why were they called Earth Band? We'd naturally assume they're from planet Earth. Unless it means they were of the soil. Sometimes I feel I am underneath the earth somewhere. It's possible. And then how would you ever find me?

It would explain the absence of light here.

YU (yours underground),

Joy

August 10—10:16 a.m.

Joy,

I'm in Melissa Vacro's house. Do you remember her? The middle-aged woman who lived by herself down the block from us? She pretty much kept to herself, and had a teenage son? It's one of the few houses in our neighborhood that hasn't become uninhabitable. Our house has long since turned into a pile of mulch. (And it just started sprouting flowers! Big red ones with huge petals.)

Melissa's house is pretty much as she left it. It's not often that you see real houses anymore. Everything has been altered so drastically; hardly anything is the way you remember it. But it's all here: her furniture, the photographs on the wall, the other signs that someone once lived here. It's like some shrine or museum left behind—a pocket of proof that humans once lived here.

I can't deny that I immediately started snooping around. Not so much because I had to know everything these people did, but more that it gave me something to do. Something to explore. There hasn't been much in the way of missions since I visited Davey for the last time.

I found some food and bottled water at least. It's so strange, the level of change that's happened. Even the labels of cans look strange and undecipherable. I never know what I'll find when I open one up. Much of the food, I don't recognize. The bottled water looks normal enough, though.

There are tons of wild plants now that appear to be edible, but I can never be sure. I try to avoid those kinds of things as much as possible, and so far I've been pretty good at scavenging food. This house has working plumbing (and electricity, naturally), but the water is a light shade of green. It's clear the tsunami affected the reservoir (and why wouldn't it?). So I'm not sure if the tap water is even safe anymore. I guess I'd have to boil it beforehand, if I wanted to use it for cooking or anything.

There was some money in one of the bedrooms upstairs, but as you can guess, money is pretty meaningless at this point. Most of the trappings of our former existence are pretty irrelevant now.

The biggest luxury is that there are actual beds to sleep on!

I can still tune in radio stations occasionally. There are few still on the air, but it sounds like things were a lot worse than originally projected. A lot more dead. Which makes sense, because I've been wandering around and haven't seen much in the way of other people. It's not completely deserted, but it's not teeming with people around here, either.

I couldn't get the cable to work, though. In the old days, you could still get channels on the television without a hook-up, but now it's just a lot of static.

Did I say the beds were the biggest luxury? It might be a toss-up. This place has a functioning bathroom as well. A shower that has hot water, and a toilet that works. You do not realize the importance of those kinds of things until you go without them awhile. The water from the shower comes in various shades of green, but I can't worry about everything anymore. It would drive me crazy to get too caught up in it.

I think I'll stay here for a few days. It's not like I have any real responsibilities these days. And I can explore some more when I need something to do. Did I tell you she has a whole bookcase full of books, too? And some of them actually look worth reading.

And I'm so sick of moving around all the time.

I wish you were here.

Aaron

August 11—3:32 a.m.

Aaron,

I'm glad you're in a safe, comfortable place. It must be nice to sleep in a bed. Heck, it must be nice to sleep. We here in the Dark Passage don't. Straw mats are taken out of the supply closet at ten o'clock every night and we put them down on the ground and lie on them with our eyes wide open. My head gets this numb feeling, like when the dentist gives you Novocaine. I'm conscious, but I feel my thoughts slowing.

If I think of a cat, for instance, I would see a close-up of fur in my mind's eye and wonder what it was, then realize it was fur, then wonder whose fur. Then maybe see a cat's paw, the torso, the neck, the head, the triangular ears, and then think, "This is a cat." It takes about an hour to reach that point and then progress painstakingly to whatever thought I had about the cat. It is almost like being drugged-out, but we are not given drugs. It is the Balloon Heads controlling our minds. If they were not so mentally powerful, they would have died weeks ago.

I've tried to talk to the Balloon Heads since I found out who they are, or rather, used to be. Because they're not those people anymore. The only thing they have in common with their former selves is that they were in charge then and they are in charge now. Rafe Dinkle used to be fond of puns and bad jokes so I tried some on him and didn't get a flicker of response.

Before I walked away from him, I said, "I don't know why you're ignoring me. You must have gotten a swelled head since the tsunami."

If he didn't laugh at that one, I figure he's a lost cause. LOL.

Bradley asked me again about Davey.

I said, "Why do you want to know?"

"I just figured it might help if you talked about it," he said.

I told Bradley Davey died in the tsunami. I figured that was the best way to get him to stop questioning me about him. Davey is the last thing I want to talk about with anybody.

Bradley looked surprised. I could tell he didn't believe me.

"When did this happen?" he asked.

"I just said, in the tsunami."

"How'd you find that out?" Bradley asked.

"My husband wrote me."

Bradley frowned and didn't say anything for a bit. Then he stood up and said, "Sorry for your loss."

He walked out before I could respond.

I'd like to write more, but I have to go lie down. The Balloon Heads are calling out to me in my thoughts.

YSDW (your sleep-deprived wife),

Joy

August 12—10:40 p.m.

Joy,

I killed someone today. Well, two people actually.

I didn't wake up this morning thinking "Maybe I'll kill someone today," but it happened regardless. I really didn't want to do it. But I had no choice.

Why am I begging for you to understand? You're the one who warned me in the first place. Not to trust anyone. And you were right.

Remember those three kids I mentioned before? They were wandering around the neighborhood one day and I came upon them. I really thought they were going to attack me that day, but they told me I was wrong. They were just in the same situation I was and they were wondering if I could spare some food. So I helped them out. Once they got some food in their bellies, any perceived threat on my part seemed to melt away. I figured I was just being paranoid, things the way they are and all.

Well, the more I thought about what you said, the more I wondered if I could really trust them, and I hid. They must have gotten tired of looking for me, because they left the next day, and I didn't see them for a while.

But they came back last night. I have a sneaky suspicion they were never too far away. That they've been watching me all this time.

I was asleep in that bed in Melissa Vacro's house—I told you all about that—when I heard some noise coming from downstairs. Things were getting smashed. Someone was wrecking the place. I remembered I'd

61

seen an aluminum baseball bat in the boy's room, so I went and got that, and I carefully made my way downstairs.

They seemed like they were waiting for me to show up. Thomas, the one with the big teeth and the buggy eyes, he had a knife and came at me with it. I smashed his head in with the bat. I was surprised how easily his head caved in. I just hit his skull like it was a baseball, and his brains just sprayed all over the wall. Like his head was an egg and I'd cracked it apart without even trying. His bloated eyes were on the carpet. The other guy, Chet, tried to grab me from behind. But I kicked him in the kneecap, hard, with my good foot, and he dropped. I kicked him in the head with my swollen foot, over and over, until he stopped trying to get up. Just to be safe, I finished him off with the bat, too. It all happened so fast that I didn't have a chance to even think about what I was doing until they were both dead.

The girl, Katie, was in the corner, looking horrified. With that oversized hand of hers, she couldn't be much help to them. She had a knife from the kitchen in her other hand, the normal one, and she was waving it around as I approached her. But I swung the bat and slammed her hand, and she dropped the knife.

She started crying then.

I came so close to crushing her head, too. It was like I was caught up in the killing and I wanted it to go on and on. I didn't want it to end. But she raised her swollen hand up off the ground, with a lot of effort, and waved it in front of me. To stop.

She begged me not to kill her. It felt good.

I found some rope and I tied her up to a chair in the kitchen. But I had no idea what to do with her. I had no desire to let her go, but I didn't really want to kill her, either. Once the adrenaline decreased in my bloodstream, I wasn't as quick to violence as I first was.

I think I might just leave her here to starve, tied to that chair, when I go.

It's times like this, I wish you were here. You would know what to do in this situation. But I teeter-totter between ending her life and doing nothing. It's always one extreme or the other. I'm just not good at balancing things out sometimes. But I've never killed someone before, either.

She seems so scared, after what she saw me do to Thomas and Chet. And in some way, I really like seeing that fear in her eyes. Because I know they thought I would be easy prey when they came back, and it makes me happy that they were wrong. That they weren't as tough as they thought they were.

She's tied up tight, and I'm tired. I think I might go upstairs and go back to sleep. She can't hurt me now. In the back of my mind, I wonder if there are more of them. If the three I saw were just the first wave of them. But I really don't think they had any other allies with them. Katie just seems too scared. Like she knows there's no one to save her.

I have no idea when you'll be writing back, so sleep is probably my best option now. I'll check email again in the morning. Let me know what you would do in this situation. I think that might be helpful.

Aaron

August 13—3:18 a.m.

Aaron,

Those guys would have killed you if you didn't kill them first. You did the right thing. You think the thing with the girl is trickier because she seems defenseless and vulnerable. But the number one rule is survival. I know that sounds like a line from a cheesy novel, but isn't it true?

This sounds awful, but I was thinking, as I read your email, "Kill that bitch!" How do you know there isn't a whole gang of them out there and, if you let her go, she'll go and tell them about you?

Remember when we had that ant problem a few years back? They were all over the house, crawling on the walls and the kitchen counters, in the bathroom and on our arms. I remember going on websites to find out how to get rid of them and I swear I remember reading somewhere that if you squashed an ant, its body would release a signal that would attract other ants. It sounded weird, but after that I couldn't crush ants anymore. I just set out bait traps or flushed them down the toilet because I was so afraid of that chemical being released.

I don't know why your story reminded me of the dead ants. But it came into my mind after reading your email. Get out of that house. Go live somewhere else. I just keep thinking about ants sending out scouts to search for prime locations. That house definitely sounds like a prime location. I hate to tell you to move, but I feel like I have to. Put a plastic bag over that girl's head or drown her in the tub. I don't care how you do it, just get rid of her.

I wouldn't hesitate to kill the people I'm with, but it wouldn't get me anywhere here. It's a different world now. We don't know how to live anymore. We have to make it up as we go along. It might be years before we find out if what we've done is right.

I guess in some ways, I'm safer than you in my little prison. But you're free so you tell me which is better? Freedom or safety? The things you tell me scare me. It makes me afraid of the outside world. It actually made me feel good to be wiping a Balloon Head's butt tonight. I thought, "As long as I do this, they won't kill me."

The Balloon Heads communicate with one another. I'm sure of it. I don't know if it's through those chirp noises or if they speak to each other's minds like they do with us. Everything is too coordinated. I can feel them watching me, despite their huge heads that droop down toward the floor and their vacant eyes that never look directly at you. I wheel Balloon Heads to and from one another. Something in my mind will tell me to put Woody next to Triple Burger. I watch, but they don't move. They don't chirp more than once or twice a half hour, so I don't know why they need to be next to each other. After a while, I'll get another signal to wheel the other away. But I can't get a clue to what went on. Their dead-looking faces are inscrutable.

SSS (Survive, survive, survive),

Joy

August 13—5:22 p.m.

Joy,

I don't know what got into me today.

I woke up and came downstairs and Katie was still tied to the chair. She was already awake and immediately started begging me to let her go. I just ignored her and went about looking for food. I found some cans of chili. Well, it tasted like chili. Better than nothing, I guess. The electricity was working—these things are always tough to predict—and I could cook on the electric stove. I even put some in a bowl for her.

I brought the bowl over, intent on feeding her. I don't know why. I'd debated releasing her arms so she could eat, and decided against it. So I figured it was just easiest to feed her myself. So I put the bowl in front of her face and start trying to spoon it into her mouth, when she spits it out and starts violently rocking from side to side, trying to topple the chair over. I reached out to steady the chair, and I saw she'd gotten one of her arms free, the one with the giant hand, and she tried to grab me. But the hand's so big, she could barely lift it, and she had a hard time getting it to respond the way she wanted it to.

So I saw this big hand reaching for me, and I reacted on impulse, without even thinking, and I punched her right in the face. It was so sudden, and so hard, it knocked her out. But I felt pretty awful afterward. I'd never hit a woman before. It just didn't feel right at all.

After that, I ate my bowl of chili. I was so hungry, I ended up eating hers, too. I figured she didn't deserve food the way she was acting. I watched her while I ate, and when I was done, I went to the cupboard and got this big cleaver. Nice, sharp piece of cutlery.

67

And then I took her clothes off. I know what you're thinking, but I wasn't going to do anything to her. I swear it. If I did, would I be telling you about this? I just wanted to see what her body looked like. How much she'd changed. I mentioned I watched them go at it before, and I was curious about seeing her up close. There were a lot of strange growths on her skin. Weird wounds that looked like they'd never heal. Her breasts were large and lumpy, the nipples cracked. It was repulsive, actually. It was strange, examining her while she sat their unconscious. It made me feel dirty.

I waited for her to wake up and, when she did, I showed her the cleaver, and she realized she was naked, and she just panicked. She tried to rock back and forth again. But this time I raised the cleaver above my head and brought it down on her wrist, severing that giant hand of hers. The hand plopped on the floor, not even twitching, and the place where her hand was just became a bleeding wound, spraying blood everywhere. Some of it got on me, too. There was this rapidly increasing puddle growing all around her, and she struggled against the rope.

I watched her bleed out for a little while, watched her lose her strength, and then I went upstairs. I took a shower while there was still hot water, changed my clothes, gathered up my stuff, and headed downstairs.

I looked in on her one last time on my way out, and she'd stopped moving. Her head was hanging down, so her chin touched her chest, and the kitchen floor was slick with blood. So I didn't go out that way. I headed for the front door.

And the guys I'd killed yesterday, their bodies were still on the carpet. What was left of them. They were mostly skeletons now, except for a few bloated tumors that had been inside them. Untouched. Like black alien pods, that's what they looked like. But the rest of them had been picked clean. And I just know it has something to do with those mirrored roaches I'd seen eating that Balloon Head's body outside.

I stepped over their bones and went out the front door.

It's still nice outside. And I just kept walking, without looking back once. The house was a nice shelter, but it's got too many bad memories now, and I just wanted to move on to somewhere new.

I'll try to leave the neighborhood again. But I don't think I'll get far. I never do.

And I find myself wondering about that stuff you'd said about other people out there, watching us. Waiting to see what happened to the three of them who I killed. And I keep expecting someone to pop up unexpectedly from behind a bush or a tree, but no one does. And for the first time in a long time, I hear birds singing. But I don't see them anywhere. Not even the headless ones with the tendrils. But from the sound, they're up in the branches above me. They've got to be. Songbirds.

It's bothering me how easy killing is becoming. That's not like me at all. And I keep picturing Katie's hand, coming free from her wrist and slapping down on the linoleum, releasing her blood, and it really bothers me that I could take another life without a second thought.

I'm changing in ways that I don't like.

So how are things where you are?

Aaron

August 14—2:50 a.m.

Aaron,

Don't feel guilty about killing Katie. They attacked you first. You do what you have to do to survive.

People here don't talk much. Most walk around with their hands clenched and their eyes wide. They walk fast and are impatient to pass, but they have nowhere to go. I mean, all they're doing is carrying out the thought directives of Balloon Heads. And none of us trust one another. Did the Balloon Heads put that into our heads?

The only ones I talk to are Bradley, Cindy, and Jose. I have to ask myself: Why am I in here with the two people I hate most in the office? Jose seems nice, but he can't speak much English and he seems fixated on Cindy. He brings her fresh fruit every morning. When we ask where he gets it, he smiles.

Bradley gets on my nerves. He is always hovering around the Balloon Heads. I asked Bradley what he is doing squatting down beside their wheelchairs. He said he is trying to find out more about them.

"What did you find out?" I asked.

"Nothing," Bradley said.

I know that is a big fat lie. He puts his head next to their big drooping ones and smiles and laughs and talks.

It used to be hot as hell here, but now the Balloon Heads keep it cold. They have the A/C running full blast 24/7. The men love it, but all us women are freezing. Sometimes, I feel lonely and the cold penetrates my bones and starts me shivering uncontrollably. The Balloon Heads

have a tendency to sweat a lot. Whereas, before, they used to have blankets around them when it was 80 fucking degrees!

Walking along the dark hallway in the cold, I pretend I'm a cavewoman in the Ice Age. Yes, I got bored with the cat motif. The ground's hard and frozen. The plants are dead. There's no fruit or vegetables to eat. Prey is scarce. We begin to feed on ourselves.

I wonder where the electricity comes from. They keep the cold air running, but they don't give us light. And the dark and the cold are the two things I hate most. Why do all the people stuck in here turn away from one another? The directives they put in my head are a comfort sometimes. I wouldn't know what to do otherwise.

There is a little man in his 60s here who always wears a red baseball cap. We call him Batshit because he is bat-shit crazy.

"Watch out for the tall men," he says. "The tall men are evil. The small women should not be with the tall men."

Bradley said some tall dude must have stolen his woman a long time ago. But maybe Batshit is onto something. Bradley is tall and I don't trust him. I told Bradley as much, but made it sound like a joke. I read somewhere that tall men make more money and get promoted more often than short men. That makes sense, because most of the bosses were tall before they became Balloon Heads. Maybe Batshit is our Cassandra?

Amazing how we go on when everything's so shitty. Why do we go on living when there doesn't seem to be anything worth living for? Can you answer that question, Aaron?

CWITIA (Cave Woman In The Ice Age),

Joy

August 14—7:42 p.m.

Joy,

I didn't go back to Melissa Vacro's house. There was some canned food in her cupboards, and I forgot to take it when I left the place. But I couldn't go back inside. I knew to enter that kitchen would mean facing Katie again. Although at this point, I'm sure the mirrored bugs would have picked her clean and there would just be a skeleton waiting for me. And her giant, severed hand on the floor. But I knew I'd see an accusing look on her dead face, condemning me for what I'd done.

I know I was justified in what I did to those people, but it doesn't make it any easier to accept that I am a killer now.

I'm back at Davey's school. Another place I swore I'd never return to. But I thought there might be food in the cafeteria, and there was. Lots of it. But it's too heavy to carry. Giant, industrial-sized cans of mashed potatoes and vegetables and spaghetti with meatballs. It's pretty awful, but food is getting scarce. Unless I become brave enough to try to eat some of the new creatures I've seen, and I'm not sure they are all that edible. I haven't seen those strange, headless peacocks in a while. It was as if they had just been passing through.

This place doesn't creep me out like it once did. No matter how much Davey disturbs me now, I know he can't leave the gymnasium. And the other children, crab-like as they are, are more pathetic than scary. As long as I stay out of certain rooms, I'll be fine. And there's a steady flow of electricity I can count on for the laptop. I've got to admit, I've become addicted to your emails. They're one of the only things I look forward to anymore.

I think Davey knows I'm here. I don't have any proof. He hasn't called out for me or anything. But there's this strange, ominous feeling, like I'm being watched somehow. And while I'm more comfortable than I was before, I'll never be completely at ease here. I might be moving on again soon.

It's raining today. A hard, green rain that sounds metallic as it clicks against the outside of the school. I'm afraid to go outside. I keep imagining the rain is like bullets and will rip me apart. I sat by the window, watching it rain, and some of the drops hit the glass and cracked it, so I retreated deeper into the building.

The principal's office, if that's where I am, has no windows. But it does have an overhead light that works. A clock that still tells accurate time (I think), and of course there's access to the Internet.

I've been reading some of your other emails today, reading them over again, and they bring me some comfort. Knowing that you're still alive and out there somewhere. I have no idea what is keeping me from you. But I'll find a way to get to you, somehow. I swear it.

That's strange about Bradley. In one of your other emails, you mentioned that he asked you how you knew about the outside world, and you told him you have been communicating with me. But you didn't tell me what his reaction was to that. Is everyone there communicating with loved ones on the outside, or only you? If there are others, then I'm at a loss, because the people I've seen have been few and far between. They once said that about a quarter of the population survived, but I haven't seen any proof of that. That's still a lot of people. Maybe in other parts of the world, they've been luckier? But some days, I seem to be the only person left alive out here.

It sounds like you've got some real characters where you are. That Batshit guy sounds nuts, and that thing you said about Jose finding fresh fruit was really strange. I have not seen anything outside that looks like fruit as we remember it. The plant life that thrives looks malformed and alien to me. I'm too afraid to try to eat any of it. I'm sure it would poison me.

I had a vivid dream last night. I was cutting Katie's hand off over and over. And each time it hit the ground it was bigger and bigger, until it

76

filled the entire house all by itself and poked out the windows with its fingers. And there was blood everywhere.

I haven't been able to sleep in a long time, so it felt really good to sleep so deeply, but I woke feeling disoriented and afraid. The dream really troubled me.

I wish I could program my dreams. I wish I could make myself dream about you instead of monster hands.

My foot is throbbing. It has been hurting an awful lot since it started raining.

Aaron

August 15—3:07 a.m.

I'm a little freaked out that you are back at Davey's school. I've been trying to forget about Davey. Is that terrible to say?

It's impossible for me NOT to think of Davey. Bradley is always throwing questions at me about our son.

"It must be rough not being able to see him," Bradley will say.

"I'd rather not talk about it."

"Of course. It must be a terribly painful topic for you."

I want to say: Well, if you know it's painful, why do you keep bringing it up? I know I'm going to eventually go ballistic on Bradley. I know he doesn't give a rat's ass about my feelings for my son. I think he's gathering intel for the Balloon Heads. I didn't even bother to correct him, and stick with my story that Davey had died in the tsunami. It's just too much effort to maintain lies anymore, and I just don't care.

I've wondered whether the Balloon Heads can "hear" our thoughts the way that we can "hear" theirs, but these questions Bradley asks make me suspect they cannot. I'm not sure that makes sense, though. They still seem to compel me to write to you.

To answer your question about the others using email: Yes, other people do use the computers. The Balloon Heads appear to have us on a schedule where each person comes into this room to email at a specific time every day. Some people come in the morning, others the afternoon and the more unlucky ones like me get woken up in the middle of the night with an urgent need to email. Only one person comes in here at a time. The allotted time seems to be 22 minutes, which always makes me think of that radio station. "You give us 22 minutes …" Are the Balloon Heads thinking that our emails will give them the world? LOL.

When I write, "I have to go now," I mean it literally. Something in my head tells me that I HAVE to leave this room. I guess that is to allow enough time for everyone to be able to use this room to send out emails. Maybe this is the only place in the building where the Internet still works. I've tried to write to you for longer periods, but I get a terrible headache and this suffocating feeling comes over me and I have to get out of this room to breathe. Sometimes, I'm on the verge of telling you certain things and my nose and throat start closing as if I'm being warned not to.

I've been having dreams, nightmares really, about Davey. The altered semi-conscious sleep state we experience here makes our dreams especially vivid. He usually appears to me in the form of a giant caterpillar. It's his evil little face on a caterpillar's body.

"Mother, why have you abandoned me?" he asks.

"Why can't you ever call me Mom?"

I usually reach out to pet his pink fuzz and he backs away as he replies: "Mother, this is the appropriate measure of the distance in our relationship."

"You're such a precocious little guy."

"You didn't answer my question, Mother."

"I didn't abandon you. I'm trapped in this building."

"You're not trapped," Davey says, "You're just hiding."

"Then tell me how to get out?"

His eyes narrow and he smiles. He has long, sharp teeth like a lion.

"Put your ear to my mouth and I'll whisper it," Davey says softly.

I start shaking and this nauseating feeling comes over me. I turn and run.

"Mommy!" Davey shouts in a babyish voice. "Mommy!"

I stop and slowly turn. I wake up from the dream.

I know it doesn't sound like much, but this dream terrifies me. I'm starting to hate going to sleep. Davey has always scared me, but from what you've told me about him, he now literally is a monster. Was it our lack of love for our child that did this to him? Sometimes I think of Davey and I go into the bathroom and vomit.

I HAVE to go. I need to breathe.

Love,

Joy

NSLATT (No silly little acronyms this time). Oops ... well, I tried ... grin ...

August 16—2:12 p.m.

Joy,

I'm bored. That's got to be the answer. Boredom.

I've taken to creating elaborate mazes for the crab children. There are more left than I first thought. Maybe around ten. They must have been hiding the last time I was here.

It's funny. I can make rooms off-limits by closing doors, so I go throughout the school, closing and opening doors at random, making intricate mazes for the children to run through.

They're less and less human these days. They have a hard enamel shell, and their hands and feet are pretty much done evolving (devolving?) into crab claws. Their heads are flattened ovals. I almost find myself wondering what they taste like. I always did love crab cakes. But I know they were human once, so I haven't crossed that line yet.

I leave them food. In the cafeteria, there are huge, industrial-sized cans of sauces and vegetables. I spilled some spaghetti sauce on the floor, a big can of it, and they came out of their hiding places to lap it up. They're not afraid of me anymore. They're used to me being around. It sure didn't take long.

When they moved away from the big red puddle, it was licked clean. They must still have human tongues. The floor was originally crusted with dirt, and that's washed away as well. I could clean all the floors of the building just by leaving a trail of spaghetti sauce.

It's nice to eat normal food, at least. Some of the things I found in abandoned houses—or what was left of them—were often strange.

Right down to the labels, like I said. Like the food transformed along with the people. And the houses, and the cars.

The school building is changing as well. I told you that. But it's even more prominent now. Here, in what used to be the principal's office, there are eyes all over the walls. Or they look like eyes. Only recently did they start to move, the pupils growing and contracting regularly, to make me believe they can actually see. The roof and walls are always creaking and I know that it's only a matter of time that this place, like our old house, falls in on itself and becomes just as organic and alive as most of the other houses around here. It's like any trace of wood has become a living creature, so that turns first, and the rest follows slowly. The more wood in the composition, the faster the change.

There are some brick houses that haven't changed much at all. Like Melissa Vacro's place. But I suspect even that house will metamorphosize over time.

What is the building you're in like? Have you examined the walls, the ceilings? Has it changed already into something alive and breathing, or is it like it was before? I wonder how much things are altered where you are, or if they've somehow stayed the same. Untouched.

But I know nothing is untouched anymore.

I've toyed with the idea of making the maze go into the gymnasium, so the last of the crab children can be devoured by Davey. I know—it's awful—but I told you I was bored. The thought of him gobbling up the rest of them is kind of amusing. I mean, they're not really children anymore. And he is hungry. I hear him call out all the time for food. Sometimes he even calls out for me. And you.

But I don't think he really believes I'm still here. He might think I left and never came back.

I'm tempted to go see him again. But I'm not that bored yet.

There is a sword on the wall behind this desk. It looks like a Civil War replica. I used to collect Japanese swords, remember? Katanas. Well, this certainly isn't one of them. The scabbard looks like something a Civil War general would have strapped around his waist.

I took it down and stabbed one of the walls this morning. It started to bleed, but it couldn't make any sounds. It's all flesh and eyes. No mouths.

Yet.

And it moved. Undulated. Like it was trying to get away from me. But it can't. It's a wall.

The blood was bright green.

I still think about those people I killed. I don't regret it as much as I used to. I almost kind of relish the memories now. Does that mean there's something wrong with me?

Am I losing my mind?

Then again, can anyone be sane in this world we're in now? This strange, unrecognizable planet that exists after the green tsunami?

Aaron

August 17—2:04 a.m.

Aaron,

Things do indeed change around here. I'd been thinking recently about Davey and children's stories we used to read to him. I remember reading the original Pinocchio to Davey and The Velveteen Rabbit. Davey asked me at the end of each why anything would want to be "real."

"You wouldn't want to be made of wood, now would you?" I asked Davey.

"I want to be made of something strong," Davey said. "Skin is soft and bleeds too easy. It would be okay to be made of wood, or to be a robot would be even better. Nothing could hurt you and you could live forever."

"But you wouldn't be human," I said.

Davey made a face. "Humans are weak," he said.

"Weak isn't always bad," I told him. "It gives you compassion for other creatures."

"That's like a kind of love, isn't it?" Davey asked.

"In a sense," I said.

"Love is gross," Davey said. "If love can turn one thing into another, can hate turn one thing into another, too?"

"I guess," I said uneasily.

Davey's face lit up. "Cool," he said. "I'd like to turn into a robot one day or a really big rock that could crush people."

"That can't happen, Honey," I said. "That's make-believe."

"No," Davey said, "You and Father will help me so I won't have to be human."

I wasn't sure what he meant and I didn't want to know, so I turned off his light and told him to go to sleep. Now that we are in this world where everything changes, it seems like these stories are coming true. Inanimate objects are becoming real and humans are turning into things. I wonder if in some way Davey is happy now that he isn't human anymore. Do you think we did this to him?

The walls here are soft like skin. They seem to bleed a sticky liquid when I touch them. I hear moans that I once thought were made by the other people in here, but now I think the walls are making that sound because I hear the moaning when I am alone here in this room. I hear sighing, too.

Remember I told you that Jose brings Cindy fresh fruit every morning and we couldn't figure out where he got it from? It turns out the people on the floor above us have been changing into something not quite human. Some sort of plant/human hybrid. Bradley told me about them. He said the Balloon Heads told him. They said we could go upstairs and pick some fresh fruit and vegetables off these creatures.

I went upstairs with Bradley and Jose. Cindy was too scared to go upstairs. They have light. It hurt my eyes. There were no Balloon Heads upstairs. I saw this guy who had a cantaloupe for a head and acorn squash for arms. His neck was made of watermelon and his stomach was full of grapes. His legs were still human legs and a pair of eyes peered out of his melon head. He had a mouth and teeth and a tongue. None of these people wore clothes.

Jose had a knife and he cut the melon head off the watermelon neck. The guy screamed as the knife went through him. He screamed for a few minutes and then went silent. Jose told me that their heads and other parts grow back every day, so it should be an inexhaustible food source.

Bradley and Jose had this big bucket with them to collect the fruit and vegetables and they went around lopping bits off the hybrids. The screams didn't bother them. It made me sick. When I threw up, Bradley and Jose laughed.

Bradley shook his head and said, "Women."

Cindy and I refused to eat the fruit and vegetables. Cindy asked me if the fruit she ate every morning made her a cannibal. I told her no because it wasn't human flesh anymore.

I kept thinking about Pinocchio for some reason. He's real; he's not made of wood. The second floor people are not real people. They're made of pulp and seeds and stuff like that. At least that's what I tell myself. I still can't bring myself to eat them, now that I know the truth, but the fruit and veggies smell so good. Fresh and sweet. And I wonder how much longer I'll hold out before I start eating them again. Bradley and Jose say they're not human beings anymore. I wonder if they're talking about the hybrids or about themselves.

MELONcholily Yours,

Joy

August 17—8:11 p.m.

Joy,

I guess I've become Davey's accomplice. I closed all the doors, except for the gymnasium, and I chased two of those crab children down the hall. Then I stayed by the door and watched what happened next.

At first it looked like he was sleeping, over at the other end of the gym. His bulbous, misshapen body looked like it was segmented. Before, he had looked like some kind of doughy caterpillar, but now, he looks much more insect-like. Like he's transforming into some kind of centipede.

When the children wandered close enough to him—I swear those things are almost completely blind—a large segment of his body lashed out like a whip and large suction cups grabbed onto them. Their claws clattered on the hardwood floor as the suction cups opened into mouths and swallowed them whole. The entire time Davey continued sleeping.

I watched it all, fascinated by the process. I realized that Davey is no longer our son. He is some kind of monster now. I watched him like I would a nature special where a python swallows a goat.

As he digested his meal, Davey lifted his head and stared at me with glassy eyes. I don't know if he really saw me at all, or even realized that it was me who brought this food to him. Certainly, at this point, he can't hunt prey by himself. He's pretty much helpless. He'd probably have to start devouring his own body if I hadn't brought the kids to him.

I had the Civil War sword with me for protection, in case he tried to advance upon me, but he didn't. It is strange how little he looks like the Davey you would remember. He's a totally different creature at this point. Even his face has changed since the last time I saw it.

He does not appear to be aware of his surroundings, or what he has become. And he made no attempt to communicate with me.

There are about four more of the kids. And I know that I'll be feeding them to Davey soon.

It reminds me when I was a kid and I had a pet king snake and I used to feed it mice. Eventually, my mother made me get rid of it, but while I had it, I could watch that thing eat for hours.

It was fascinating stuff.

And, really, what else do I have to do?

Aaron

August 18—3:01 a.m.

Aaron,

It is hot here, again. That scares the shit out of me. I didn't like the cold and the damp, but I have to wonder—why the heat?

Cindy said earlier today, "It's a hothouse in here."

"Don't say that," I told her.

She asked why. I didn't answer. All I could think was: growth, metamorphosis, plants, seed, flowers, FRUIT. Those people on the floor above were just like us until the day they weren't. When, why, *how* did they change?

I asked Bradley why it was hot. He said he didn't know.

"But you talk to them every day," I said.

"They don't talk, Joy. You know that."

But I don't believe him. Batshit doesn't like the heat either.

"Hot weather brings bugs," Batshit said. "There's good and there's evil. The tall men shouldn't be with the short women."

"What should we do?" I asked.

"This," Batshit said, and he started licking the walls.

That's when the moaning started. It sounded like two people having sex. I put my hand on Batshit's throat and felt the vibration. I touched the wall. It was purring like a cat. I closed my eyes, the feeling drawing me in. One hand on Batshit's throat, the other on the wall. The heat was like a volcano. I started sweating. Then tingling.

I opened my eyes. The Balloon Head, Woody, was watching me.

"STOP!" Bradley shouted.

He ran over and pulled me away from the wall. Batshit was still licking and moaning. His face melting like a wax candle. I wanted to go over and help him, but Bradley held me back.

"We need you," Bradley whispered in my ear.

We stood and watched Batshit drip. Little by little, he became less and less until there was nothing but a puddle on the floor. Jose came with a mop and wrung what was left of Batshit into a big, black bucket and wheeled him away.

A little while later, Bradley came into the room carrying a red milk crate full of baby bottles. We all knew what we had to do. We each took a bottle and fed a Balloon Head. I stuck the nipple into Woody's mouth. It reminded me of when Davey was a baby. Remember how the suckling noises made me want to vomit?

Cindy asked me, "That was Batshit, wasn't it?"

I didn't answer.

Somebody shouted, "Put on the A/C. I'm dying here."

I touched my face. I didn't feel any change. I'm touching it still as I'm writing this. I'm the same. I haven't changed, Aaron. It's just sweat.

Volcanically Yours,

Joy

August 18—1:35 p.m.

Joy,

I almost killed Davey today.

I'd sent the last of the crab kids his way, through the maze of the hallway, the only open door leading to the gymnasium. And, as always, Davey drew them to him and closed up on them and devoured them whole with his body.

I stood there in the doorway, with that rusty Civil War sword I'd found, and I pictured in my mind bringing that sword down on him over and over again, slicing him open, slicing him apart. He isn't really Davey anymore. I know that. He's something else. And the way he feeds on everyone around him nauseates me.

So, why not put him out of his misery?

He finally noticed me there. Like I told you, I think his eyesight is failing. Something to do the metamorphosis he's going through, no doubt. But he stared at me as he digested those human crabs.

"Daddy," he said.

And I thought about all the problems he'd given us. All the headaches, the bad behavior. And I know he's always been a bad seed. He's always had a great potential for evil. And I really don't want to believe that you and I created such a person.

But he's still our son. And he sounded so helpless. So much like a child.

"That's the last of them," I told him. "The school is empty now. Just you and I."

He just stared, looking sad, as those suction cups and mouths on his elongated body did their work.

"What do we do now?" I asked him.

"I don't know," Davey said. "I don't want to be like this anymore."

And for the first time, he showed real regret. In the past, when he would apologize for something, it never seemed sincere. He always seemed to be playacting. But this time, I could tell he was telling the truth. He didn't like being an overgrown monster who devoured his peers.

So I walked closer to him. I gripped the hilt of the sword hard, ready to use it at a moment's notice. But he didn't make a move to grab me.

I knew it was only a matter of time, though. Once he digested his last victims, and started to get hungry again. I would look more and more appetizing to him.

"What do we do now?" I asked him again.

"I don't know, Daddy," he said. "I don't want to stay here anymore. I don't like it here."

I was thinking of moving on myself. Not so much because of him, but because the building was starting to become more and more alive, and in the process had become more and more unstable. Some rooms simply collapsed on themselves, the floors and ceilings merging into new appendages I'd never seen before.

The principal's office, where I'd been staying, was making stranger and stranger noises, and I started to feel this psychic pull. That's the only way I can describe it. Beckoning me to come closer to the walls with all the eyes. To become one with whatever the school was changing into.

I didn't want to stay there anymore, either.

So what was I to do? Finish Davey off completely? Leave him there to starve to death? Or did I have another option? A way for us to go our separate ways?

I realized then I couldn't kill him. Not willingly. Not unless he attacked me somehow. I'd gone into that room so intent on finishing him off.

Of bringing all of this to a close, and then, when I had to face him, my plans just disintegrated.

"I'm leaving," I said. "You should leave, too. There's no more food for you here."

And instantly I thought of what his "food" would entail. Outside these walls, he'd still seek out living, moving prey. Whatever he could get a hold of. If I let him out of this place, he would become a dangerous predator out there. Could I release such a thing on the unsuspecting world?

Then again, it was all so strange now. It wasn't my world anymore.

As long as he didn't try to eat me, I didn't see much reason why I shouldn't let him go.

"Daddy," he said. "How do I get out?"

At the other end of the big room, there were two double doors. I walked down to them and opened them. I kicked down the rubber stoppers that would keep them open. Together, the two doorways made a good-sized exit for a victorious basketball team, or a monster like Davey.

"Can you fit through there?" I asked him.

"I don't know," he said.

I was going to offer to help him. But the truth is, I couldn't bring myself to touch him. I didn't want to even go near him any closer than I had to.

"Try," I said. "Can you move on your own?"

"Yes, I think so. But I haven't moved much in a long time, except to eat."

He tried to move toward the doors. I didn't see any feet, but there must have been some kind of appendages beneath him. His big, bulky body crawled slowly toward the way out.

The way he moved bothered me. I started to feel sick. So I left the gym.

I went back to the principal's office, and gathered my things. What little I still carry around with me. A backpack and a bag with the laptop.

I went to the kitchen and looked for food I could take with me, but most of it was those big, industrial-sized cans. That's why I hadn't plundered the kitchen the last time I was there. Giant cans of green beans. Corn. Chili with meat.

There wasn't a lot I could carry without weighing myself down. But there were candy bars. Granola bars. Things like that were loose, or in boxes. I gathered up as many I could fit into my backpack. And some bottles of water.

The backpack was heavy, but I'd be able to handle it.

And I held onto the sword.

When I was all packed and ready to go, I went back to the gymnasium, to see what Davey's progress was. But he was already gone.

Some weird chunks of flesh hung to the exit doors, still moving and alive. I guess he'd had a hard time fitting through, but he figured it out.

He was free.

So I left in the opposite direction.

Aaron

August 19—3:01 a.m.

Aaron,

I'm not sure why, but I'm glad you let Davey out. After reading your email, I daydreamed that Davey used his massive body to break into this place. He ate all the Balloon Heads and set everyone free. I jumped on Davey's back and lay on my stomach, hugging his sticky, bloated body. He smelled like rotted potatoes.

This little boy I never felt comfortable around—whom, deep down in the darkest part of my heart, I wished would go away—I'm now having heroic fantasies about. It should be the parent rescuing the child, not vice versa. Yet thinking about his monstrousness and how it might benefit me in this bizarre new world gave me a perverse feeling of pleasure.

Yes, I am the world's worst mother. No wonder Davey turned out like this.

I finally gave up (or is it gave in?) and ate a piece of second floor fruit. It's so hot and the watermelon was so juicy and cool, I had to put my mouth on it and then once my mouth was on it and I tasted its sweetness, I had to take it inside me and swallow it. I guess I am the same as Davey swallowing those little children. I also ate a plum and a banana. Cindy still wouldn't take a bite even though she ate the fruit when she didn't know where it came from. The way she looked at me when she saw me eating the watermelon hurt my feelings.

Why are there always people who think they're better than everyone else? I never liked Cindy's moralistic shit. But these past couple of weeks, I felt like we bonded, and now I'm feeling like she hacked off a part of me.

I don't know that there's anyone left now besides Cindy, who's not eating the fruit. It's funny about the walls, isn't it? I didn't know you felt the pull too. People here sometimes rub themselves against the walls in a sexual way. There's a musky odor that I didn't smell before. Woody perks right up when he sees people at the wall. Normally, the Balloon Heads are droopy and lethargic. But I don't think there's anything droopy going on inside their heads.

I'd like to melt away like Batshit. The wall is tempting me. Bradley seems to sense when I feel the pull because he'll usually call to me to come talk to him or do something for one of the Balloon Heads. I like pushing them around in their wheelchairs; I like bathing and feeding them. It gives me a purpose.

We give the Balloon Heads a bottle almost every morning. I don't notice if there's any people missing. They all seem to blend into this single entity: the faceless crowd. I don't feel like a person anymore. Maybe that's how I am able to eat the fruit.

But I'm still breathing and if there's breath, there's hope. I don't know if I made that up or if it's one of those 'truisms.' Truisms are funny because they're not always true.

Good luck with wherever your journey leads. Do you think we'll ever find each other? Or Davey?

LWOA (love without acronyms),

Joy

August 19—8:11 p.m.

Joy,

I don't know if I mentioned the buzzing to you before, but there was this loud, overwhelming hum that would come and go. It never lasted long, but it was disconcerting (yes, something can be disconcerting, even in this new world where everything seems that way).

Well, I think I finally found the source.

As I tried to make my way toward the city (again), I came across something that shocked me. The only way to describe them was giant bugs. Man-sized insects. Big, black beetles with large, segmented eyes like large red globes on their heads. Their appearance filled me with a strong sense of repulsion, more than they should have. I mean, they were creepy enough, but they bothered me in a way I can't quite put my finger on, down to the core of my being.

And yet, at the same time, I felt compelled to approach them, to touch them. It's funny how I seem to have such little control over my impulses anymore.

At that time, they were not buzzing. But I assumed they had to be the cause.

In fact, as I stood there, reaching out to feel their hard carapaces, they were completely still. Not even any sign of breathing (how would one tell through such a hard exoskeleton?). I wasn't even sure if they were real or if they were statues.

But I was convinced they were alive, because of the sudden, strong, repellent sensation I got as I touched them.

I forced myself to move away from them. I was about five feet away, staring at them, waiting for them to move. But they didn't.

And then, suddenly, I felt a great throbbing in my gigantic foot. A pain that caused me to lose my balance and tumble to the ground, flailing around as I tried to get my bearings. It was so unexpected. I sat there in the dirt, hugging my foot to me, waiting out the pain with tears in my eyes. It finally subsided and I was able to stand again.

I then moved as far away from those creatures as I could.

I know there is something important about them. That they play a role in the events that have transpired. But I have no clue as to what that role might be.

Have you ever seen such a thing where you are?

It is like they just suddenly sprouted from the earth. I'd never seen their like before. But now they stand there, like ancient monoliths.

I have no idea what they are, but they have been haunting my nightmares. Last night, I dreamt that several of them had me trapped and were eating me alive.

Of all the odd things I've seen, of all the threats I've confronted so far, these have been the most troublesome to me. And I have no idea why.

Aaron

August 20—3:03 a.m.

Hey Aaron,

No, I have never seen such bugs as you describe. I doubt that they are of any relevance at all. I would not disturb them if I were you, for you might end up being very, very sorry.

I am wondering if you have any idea where Davey is. I imagine in his present humongous form, he is difficult to overlook. Perhaps you could ask if anyone has seen him? I do feel that he has the power to locate my position and deliver me from this underground dreariness.

Today, I ate a peach. It was sweet and juicy. The fuzz on it felt warm and human. Much like I would imagine it to feel if I brushed my cheek against one of those fur-faced old ladies I used to see on the bus. They couldn't have survived the tsunami, could they? The way they used to ride the bus back and forth all day and not go anywhere, I couldn't see the point to their being alive.

The peach gave me energy and it made me smile all day long. I even smiled at "my" Balloon Head, Woody. Cindy is still not eating the fruit. She is weak and sick, yet the moral smugness remains. As she scowled at me while I ate the peach, I found myself wondering what type of fruit she'd turn into. I think she might end up a freeze-dried fig.

I heard rumors the third floor is all vegetables now. Perhaps Bradley will go upstairs with me, as I am dying for a corn on the cob. It is wonderful to have fresh food again. I cannot help but feel grateful to the Balloon Heads, for I am sure they had something to do with the transformation. I wish I knew the formula for how this is done. Then I could tell you and you could enjoy delicious, fresh fruit, too.

There is a little child here now. It looks to be about two or three years old. I can't tell if it's a boy or a girl. Bradley thinks that someone from the second floor, amid the human-to-fruit change, got Jose to take pity and bring it down here. It seems likely, as Jose has been feeding it like a stray kitten. We are all a little wary of it, as we don't know if the child could infect us with this fruit disease. Some people are talking about taking it back upstairs, but nobody is brave enough to touch it. Jose claims he never touched the child and he doesn't know how it got here.

The tyke is annoying. It screeches and mewls like a sick cat. Even if it is not infected, I wish it would go away. I think Cindy wants to pick it up and comfort it, but she is afraid of what the others will do if she does.

It is screeching now somewhere in the hall. And it is 3 a.m. I loathe its big, round, wet eyes, its snot-dripping, walnut-shell of a nose. Its curly black hair is greasy and looks like it's been applied to its head by a paint roller. I wish Davey were here so I could feed it to him.

I need to eat another peach. I'm starting to get depressed again.

August 20—11:46 a.m.

Joy

How you can say the bugs have no relevance? How can either of us know what is and isn't important anymore? The world is so different now.

I've seen these creatures at various points throughout the neighborhood. They usually stand in groups of two or three, and I swear they weren't there before. I have no idea where they came from. There aren't a lot of them, but the ones there are look ominous to me. I have yet to catch them buzzing. When I hear the noise and go to see if it originates with them, the sound stops. But I know they are the source. They *have* to be.

I have the strangest feeling that they are waiting for something to happen. And I'm not sure if I want to know what.

Your stories about fruit make me hungry. I don't care what the origins of them are. They sound better than what I've been able to scavenge. Much of the food left behind has gone bad or mutated in strange ways. As for food growing in the "wild," I have no idea what is edible and what's not anymore, but I'm getting more and more inclined to risk it. At least you know what you're eating is safe and it doesn't hurt you.

The school building caved in upon itself. Now it looks like a vast green lump. Almost like clay. The windows, that had changed to strange eyes made of glass, are now completely gone. If anything remained alive in there, it must be suffocated by now.

I have no idea where Davey is. After he got out of the building, he moved surprisingly fast on the outside, considering how large he has grown. I lost sight of him fairly quickly. To tell you the truth, I'm in no hurry to see him again. I don't like what he has become. And I won't go out of my way to find him. But I wish him luck surviving out there, in this new world.

That toddler you saw sounds as disturbing as Davey. What kind of world turns children into monsters?

Well, the power here is running low. I'd better sign off now.

I'll try to write again soon.

Aaron

August 21—2:46 a.m.

Aaron,

Tonight, this naked dude was rubbing his dick against the wall. I don't really know too many people here. I keep to myself. But I knew him because I gave him a nickname: Jockohama. I called him that because all he ever talked about was sports. That seemed ridiculous to me. All the ball players are probably dead or transformed to the point of losing all athletic ability. And there's no place to watch players play anymore.

Jockohama interested me because I wanted to see at what point he'd finally stop talking about sports and see that he was part of an increasingly shrinking group of survivors of the worst calamity on earth. Well, like the song says, tonight's the night. He had his arms and legs pressed on the wall like a gecko. And he was rubbing the dick like a horny dog on a table leg. It was almost funny.

Jockohama was moaning. As I continued watching, he started making the type of noise you make when you walk on hot sand in your bare feet in the middle of summer. His dick looked like a popsicle melting in the sun. The ooze ran down the wall and onto the carpet. I heard this clattering noise and turned around and saw Jose rolling his bucket and mop toward the melting man.

I felt sick and ran down this dark passage where I go hide. I heard sniffling and saw the child sitting in my corner. I shined a flashlight on it, hoping to scare it away. Its face had become long, red, and heart-shaped with little black specks. I had such a craving for something sweet, I dug my nails into its face and scooped out some pulpy flesh. It was the perfect strawberry. Not tart at all and it was juicy. I ate its face. When I was done, the headless child got up and ran away. I don't know

111

how it is alive without a head. All I could think was, "At least I won't have to hear you cry anymore."

What are you doing out there, Aaron? Why aren't you trying to find me? Things here are getting worse. We're dying here. If it's not the fruit, it's the walls that get you. And all you can talk about are those damn buzzing bugs. Fuck those bugs. What about me, your wife?

Now I remember what it was that we were fighting about before the tsunami hit. It was about your obsession with minutia. How you were so involved with things that you couldn't see me, you couldn't see Davey. Maybe that's why Jockohama stood out to me. He was so focused on sports, nothing else existed. I wanted to yell at him, "Hey, asshole, it's the end of the fucking world."

Just like I wanted to yell at you, "Do you see me? Can you hear me? Do I exist? Do you care?"

And now, I say to myself, Aaron isn't going to find me. He just wants to look at the funny bugs. Maybe that's why I kept fantasizing about Davey, of all people, rescuing me.

I'm sorry if this hurts you, but I just threw up the baby's strawberry head. There are red guts all over the laptop and my fingers are bleeding strawberry juice.

Very Truly Yours,

Fucking Joy

August 21—2:44 p.m.

Joy,

Remember me telling you how my foot throbs unbearably every time I try to leave the neighborhood? Well, I noticed my foot doesn't hurt much anymore. Ever since I had that bad pain attack near those bugs. It's like that was the last of it.

I don't know why I felt the impulse, but I tried to walk out of the neighborhood this morning, and nothing stopped me. It will still take me awhile to get there, but at least it's a start. I wasn't going to say anything because I don't want to jinx this. I don't know if there are other barriers between here and where you are. I didn't want to get your hopes up. But it sounds like you're about to give up on me. And I wanted to make it clear that I'm still trying.

There aren't many other people. Not that I've seen. The ones I have come across are deformed in weird ways and won't come out of their hiding places, but I see them watching me. And what I see of them makes me think that my foot was one of the more merciful mutations. The good news about that is at least nobody has tried to attack me again.

I have this small transistor radio. It was tossed in a drawer years ago and we forgot all about it. But, except for the laptop, it's my only contact with the world outside here. It sounds like many of the people who are left are moving south, to Los Angeles. Maybe we should go down there, too.

It's funny. The guy on the radio today was talking about the tsunami. About how it felt when it came. Do you remember that? One minute, it was just another day, and the next, there was this huge wave blocking

113

out the sky, crashing down on us. Not like rain at all. Smashing most of the buildings. Drowning millions of people. And yet, some of us survived. I have no idea why we didn't perish with the rest of them. Our measly little house wasn't any stronger than the skyscrapers the tsunami crashed to ruins.

I was home. The wave should have pulverized the house. I should have drowned. But I didn't. And our house was mostly whole, even as it slowly disintegrated upon itself, becoming a big, breathing lump of alien flesh. A new life-form. One that didn't provide shelter for creatures like us anymore.

The guy on the radio was talking about this. How could anything have lived through that?

It's almost like the tsunami was alive, too. Like it spared some of us on purpose.

There's damage, but not everything is damaged. And it's selective. You'll see a house that looks untouched in the middle of other houses that were smashed to bits.

I don't claim to understand any of this.

The truth is, I can't remember much of what happened after the wave crashed down on me. I remember struggling in liquid, a helpless, drowning sensation, and that's about it. The next thing I knew, I was stretched out on our lawn, near the garden. Whole, and barely wet. Just that green film covering me. Even the ground was mostly dry by then.

Have I told you how quickly the water had disappeared afterward? Sucked into the earth? Into the sky? I have no idea. No one does. It left as quickly as it arrived.

The people in Los Angeles. Supposedly there are only about fifty of them there, but it's more people in one place than I've seen in what seems like ages. There was a broadcast from there. It sounded like most of them were praying. I guess the end times are finally here. But I refuse to believe this was some kind of biblical prophecy come to life. None of this makes sense. There are no angels here to take people away. Just a lot of drowned, dead bodies, especially along the shorelines. That's what I heard.

114

I found a store with some fresh batteries and snagged a bunch. Between the radio and the laptop, I can't afford to lose my only connections with the outside world.

I'm coming. I'm trying to get to you.

I just don't know if I'll be able to get that far. Or if something will stop me.

Aaron

August 22—2:22 a.m.

Aaron,

What are we doing on this fucked up planet? Why are we alive when so many are dead? I guess the dead have always outnumbered us. The Silent Majority, I believe they were once called—well, until Nixon hilariously appropriated the term to describe Americans who were not a part of the counterculture. I guess one could interpret that as meaning conservative people are dead. LOL. I must tell Bradley that one. Although conventional politics hardly matter now. And Bradley's new focus is the Balloon Heads. He still crouches down to chat with them every day.

I couldn't help but think of Darwin when you wrote of the randomness and illogic of who did and didn't survive the tsunami. Is it luck or is there an intelligent force behind this? I always fall back to the Balloon Heads. I'm sure they have some role in deciding who lives and who dies. Why are some people destroying themselves on the wall and one floor turns to fruit and another to veggies (rumor has it)? I think the Balloon Heads give us these irresistible impulses to melt into walls, to get up at 2 a.m. to write on a laptop, to tear off and consume the head of a strawberry child.

The child is still creeping around with no head. It can't vocalize anymore, but we can still hear it as it crashes into things. A common occurrence now that it can no longer see. People were asking what happened to its head, but nobody knew. Bradley looked at me and smirked the first time that question was asked. I'm too ashamed to ask him what he knows. The child is a brutal reminder to all who are parents here. But nobody speaks of loved ones.

117

I want to bring you up and say, "Aaron says this and Aaron says that." But I stop myself and think *What if no one else can communicate with their spouse? What if the other people's emails went unanswered?* Nobody talks about it, so there's no way to know. If I say something, there's a good chance some people would resent me, and I don't want to upset someone. So we've intuitively made this into a taboo topic.

Cindy is always lying down on her straw mat. She's running a fever and barely has the strength to get up to go to the bathroom. I was mad at her for not eating the fruit, but now I just feel sad. I put cold washcloths on her forehead and lay her head on my lap and pet her long, silky blonde hair. Well, it is not so much silky now as it is greasy. I try to bathe her every few days, but she is so weak that it exhausts her. I want to feed her some of the fruit because I know it will help her, but she keeps saying no. She clutches at the stuffed donkey Jose gave her like a little girl.

"I'll die before I eat that," Cindy said, staring up at me from my lap.

"You will die then," I said.

"What's to live for?" Cindy asked.

That shocked me, coming from Cindy. She was always the bubbly one in the office. She liked to talk about the power of positive thinking and how God wants us to spread joy in the world (joy, haha…that is definitely not me).

Cindy opened her watery, bloodshot eyes wide and said hoarsely, "The Rapture."

"Jesus is coming down here?" I asked.

"You know it's the end of the world, "Cindy said.

I gently lifted her head from my lap and left her lying on the straw mat. Do you think it's the end of the world, Aaron? I mean, we all talk about it like it is, but deep down, do we really believe it?

Spreading the Joy,

Joy

August 24—5:16 p.m.

Joy,

I am making the most progress I have in weeks, but it's been slow going. And I don't always have access to the Internet, so I've been quiet awhile. No matter how used to my foot I get, it's still a big impediment. It makes it difficult to do just about anything.

One thing that surprised me today was that I noticed the sky was turning blue again. I think it has been going in that direction all along, but I just didn't notice. It almost makes me think that things could go back to the way they were, even though I know it's too late for that.

I have seen more people now. All I can guess is that they were in the same predicament I was, where I had limited mobility, and now we all seem to have been set free. I still see groups of the giant bugs along the way, but I try to stay as far away from them as I can.

I've taken on a few traveling companions. Not something I would consciously do. I just want to get downtown and find you. But they kind of latched on to me. There's a guy named Herb whose partner is also in one of the buildings downtown. And a woman named Angela, who just wanted to get away from her neighborhood, and finally figured out she could.

They've both got deformities that slow them down. Herb has a growth on his back, like a hunchback. Angela has elongated facial features, her nose and ears hang almost to the ground. And she looks pregnant but swears she isn't. I don't know how anyone could tell anymore. Our bodies are all so changed now.

Both of them are slower than I am. I've actually gotten used to hobbling around. I want to just move at my own pace, but I feel guilty leaving them behind. Another aspect of Angela's face is that she can't see very well. I think the corneas are overgrown as well. Herb has taken a very protective attitude toward her, and I can't help but feel the same.

But I want to find you so badly.

Of course, we still have a dilemma ahead of us. You say you're not changed, and you're trapped inside the building. Does this mean coming outside could harm you? If you breathe the same air the Balloon Heads do, I'm guessing you'd be just fine. But I'm afraid to test my theory out.

And I'm sure your building is a lot different now. It might not be as easy to get into as we think.

But I can't worry about these things now. I have to get to you, and then we'll figure out a solution.

The terrain is so different now. The asphalt is covered over in plants and flowers. Cars and trucks have become strange, oversized animals that can barely move. I've been thinking about trying to kill one of them. I wonder if they're edible. But I can't see how, if they used to be metal.

I better sign off. Herb wants to see if he can reach his life partner, Jacob. I guess he's an executive in one of the firms in the city. He says no one responds to his emails, but he wants to keep trying. And who knows how long we'll have the wireless signal.

Aaron

August 25—2:12 a.m.

Aaron,

I am shaking and my skin is breaking out in goose bumps. I am so happy to get this email from you. I didn't know what the cause of your silence was? Maybe you were mad at something I wrote that made you think I was a horrible, immoral, disgusting person. How do I know how I am anymore? How do I know what is right and wrong anymore? You could have been sick or dead. I don't know if that would have been worse than you hating me. Well, I guess that is terribly self-centered of me to write that. Sorry.

Whenever I don't hear from you, I always think the worst. In this apocalypse, who can blame me? Never have you been dearer to me than in my darkest hour. It was so easy to take each other for granted in our former world of well-being. This is what love was made for, that strong steel rope that will pull us out of the hole. I gripped it so tight, my hands are cut and bleeding.

Cindy has ceased to be who she was. I guess she is dead because when you die, your physical essence is metamorphosized, and she turned into a pile of Spanish moss. I'm glad she was nothing edible, for I might have eaten her. I strung her around the corners of the straw mat I sleep on.

Her fever got worse and she'd stopped eating. I tried to give her water, but she couldn't even hold that down. I was caring for her day and night against the wishes of the Balloon Heads, who wanted the same care I was giving to her. It gave me terrible migraines to go against the thoughts they put in my head. Bradley was angry. He told me to stop wasting my time and said Cindy brought it on herself by not eating the

123

fruit. I think Bradley was scared when he saw I had the strength to fight the Balloon Heads.

He said, "You're using your power in the wrong way, Joy. You need me to help you."

"Shut up and go wipe Tomato's ass," I told him.

Cindy couldn't stop shivering until the last few hours. She stopped shivering and her fever cooled down. I thought she was getting better. I called Jose over. He looked down at her and shook his head. He'd been keeping his distance since she'd refused the fruit. I think that hurt his feelings in some way and he took it like Cindy rejected him.

As her body grew cold, I became worried, but no one would help me. Everyone acted like they couldn't see or hear me. She looked at me with her red eyes, her body a limp bag of bones, her greasy blonde hair coming out in clumps, and I thought how terrible it must feel to be her. She couldn't speak, but she looked at me like she had a question she wanted to ask. Then she lifted her head slightly and let out a powerful sneeze that was as loud as an ambulance siren. This white powdery stuff came out of her nose and covered her whole body, like something alive. Like a swarm of bees. When it dissolved, all that was left of Cindy was the Spanish moss.

The little donkey doll was still lying there, so I took it and stuffed it inside my shirt. I wanted to believe that Cindy gave it to me, that that was the question she was asking, "Will you take care of my little donkey for me?"

So Cindy isn't here anymore. And you're not here and it seemed like forever since you emailed me, and I thought, "He's never going to come for me."

I went into my hiding place and cuddled the toy donkey like I was nine years old. After a little bit, the headless child stumbled in noisily. It seemed to sense my presence and crept uncertainly toward me like a scared animal. I just sat there, seeing what it would do. It came and put its stubby arms around me.

I picked it up and threw it hard against the wall. I am so sick of monstrous, suffering creatures. I don't know if it's still alive or not, or even if that thing can be killed.

Aaron, when are you coming to take me away from this? I don't know how much more I can stand. The next thing I try to kill will be myself.

Joy

August 26—1:51 a.m.

Joy,

I'm sorry I was silent for so long. For some reason, the closer I get to you, the harder it is to maintain a signal. You would think it would the opposite. I am approaching what once was a real city. If there are any wireless signals available, you'd think the most would be where you are. But that hasn't been the case.

Or maybe my laptop is finally dying. Or *transforming*.

I'm relieved that I am finally getting closer to where you are. It was tough hearing from you in our old neighborhood and being trapped there, unable to search for you. But now that I'm finally making the journey, it's been such slow going. Part of it is my foot, which doesn't hurt like it used to, but which still slows me down considerably. The other part is the terrain, which has changed drastically.

Do you remember all those movies and books about the end of the world? In those, the world is always a desolate, barren place. Like in the aftermath of a nuclear war. Who would have thought the opposite would happen? Everything is alive and growing, even things that were inanimate before, and expanding with their transformations. Some plants have run amok and are difficult to get through. Automobiles and homes are now half plant/half animal creatures that are mostly harmless, but provide further obstacles. This also makes it difficult for me to know if I'm going in the right direction. Nothing is as I remember it.

In many ways, it's all so beautiful. So alive. Except for humans. There are hardly any of us around anymore. And those who are left are deformed and ugly. It's clear to me that we don't belong here anymore.

127

Luckily, I salvaged a compass, and it works. The earth is still upon its axis and North is still North, even though it may not look like it.

I want so badly to take you away from that place, but I have to find it first. And I have no idea how strange a landscape the city will be.

Aaron

August 26—4:02 p.m.

Joy,

Well, I saw Davey again. It wasn't the joyful reunion I'd hoped for (obvious sarcasm on my part).

I was with the others, trying to make our way through thick, twisted walls of wood that had once been trees, and we were trying to get over, when something raced at us. Something large, long, and segmented. I was sure it was some monstrous centipede, come to devour us alive, and I was partly right.

It was Davey, transformed still further. He is no longer awkward and clumsy. Now he has adapted to his new body and is quite adept at moving about quickly and accurately. His skin has taken on an even more shell-like density, and his face has grown further from what it was, and is part of a grotesque parody of a human head. Somehow I was still able to recognize him. Despite his further metamorphosis, he is still covered in large, bulbous tumors, and layers of suction cups. It's quite disturbing to behold.

He can use his body as a whip, and he immediately lashed out at Angela, knocking her to the ground. I was halfway up the wall, and dropped down, intent on helping her, but he lashed out again, knocking me out of the way. Then he wrapped his tail around her, attaching a hundred suction cups to her. Davey sucked every nutrient from her body, leaving her a brittle husk, like a bag of twigs. Her pregnant stomach, which she always claimed was not a child at all, was the only part of her body left intact, a large globe of flesh in the middle of an ossified corpse. As if it was a pit to be discarded after eating a peach.

I got to my feet and tried to confront him. I knew it was our son, even if on some level I wasn't completely convinced, and began to shout at him to leave us alone.

"I have spared your life, Daddy," he said inside my head, no longer using his human voice. "Be thankful for that. I could have just as easily devoured you instead. But, where mother rejected me from my earliest memories, I remember you showing me episodes of kindness, and now I repay those in turn."

I tried to reason with him and explain that the person he just killed was my friend, but he would have none of it. The word friend no longer had meaning for him. Luckily, Herb had already made it over the wall and was on the other side, out of Davey's view.

"I will try not to eat you," Davey said to me. "But I cannot promise anything. All I can promise is that I will save you for last. That I will try to resist until the very end."

And then, as quickly he had come, he was gone, a rapidly moving serpent crawling at top speed through the newly green world.

I knew he meant what he said. That he would try to avoid killing me for as long as he could. But I also know that humans were now his food. And who could say how many were still around. I can count the ones I've seen since leaving the neighborhood on two hands. That may sound like a lot compared to what I saw when I was trapped, but it's still not much. If Davey eats one a day, they will disappear quickly.

And then I would be his last meal before he either adapted to another food source or perished himself.

After Davey had left, I checked Angela's remains and that peach pit stomach of hers that Davey had not devoured. It was black and smooth, and resisted any attempts I made to break it open.

Herb is scared and seems to know his days are numbered. I still have the sword, but Davey's attack was so sudden that I was unable to use it. Strangely, I have not seen any working guns since the tsunami. The few I've come across have mutated into strange, half-amphibious life-forms that are completely useless.

Now I will have to be more vigilant.

Even now I can feel him watching us.

Just so you know, Angela and Herb were both sending emails out when they could. I wanted them to try to contact their loved ones as well. But neither had received a response. I hope Angela doesn't, now that I'd have to bear the news of her death. But what this means is that only you, out of many people we've tried to contact, has replied and provided proof they were still alive.

All the more reason why I am determined to save you.

We can go to Los Angeles. It will be a long trip down the coast, but it's a goal. And even if everyone there has turned into religious zealots bent on begging God's forgiveness for what we surely must have done wrong to bring about such a merciless end, it would be good to be around people again.

At least that's what I tell myself. I'm really not so sure.

Believe me, if you disagree, I am sure you could convince me otherwise.

I will try to write again as soon as I can.

Aaron

August 27—2:20 a.m.

Aaron,

After reading your last email, it gave me hope that you might actually find me. That frightens me. It's not that I don't want to see you again. But to leave this place, horrible as it is, would be a huge leap into the unknown. I haven't been outside since the tsunami hit. I don't know what to expect or if I'll be able to survive out there. I keep thinking about the Balloon Heads saying the air outside is poisonous. That is probably a lie to keep us from trying to escape, but what if it's true?

I don't even know if it's possible for you to find me. I think this building, despite its multiple floors, is underground now. I am not sure how many floors the building has; there are no windows here. But I am certain there are at least three floors. There are no working elevators, so we have to climb debris-ridden stairs, so it's not easy to advance to other floors. Remember I told you of the rumor about vegetable people on the third floor? Bradley, Jose, and I tried to go up to the third floor, but we weren't able to get past this huge concrete block that was in the middle of the stairwell. There are concrete pieces all over the stairwells, as if chunks of the building had fallen in, yet there are no holes in the floors or ceilings. Maybe they grew back after they fell out?

Your encounter with Davey sounded horrible. I wonder why he hates me so much more than you. That did hurt my feelings, reading what he said about me. I guess he wouldn't hesitate to eat his own mother? And to think I had dreams of him rescuing me. Sometimes I wish I could speak to him one last time, but what would we have to say to each other?

133

I still have Cindy's Spanish moss around my bed and I keep the stuffed donkey with me all the time. I don't know why I miss her, but I do. I guess she was the closest thing to a friend I had down here.

People are still melting on the walls. They can't help themselves. There's plenty of that white goo to bottle-feed the Balloon Heads for the next month. If everyone eventually died on the wall, how would the Balloon Heads survive? I asked Bradley and he just smiled and said something about "survival of the fittest." He definitely knows more than he's saying. I wish I could get him to confide in me.

That headless kid is still running around here, believe it or not. I don't know how it survives. How is it able to eat without a head? People have lost their patience with that thing. They have taken to throwing apple cores and melon rinds at it. Yes, we still have the fruit. I don't know what we'll do when we run out of fruit. I hope you'll get here before that happens.

I tried to squat down beside Woody and talk to him like Bradley does. I got no response, so I started talking dirty to him and Woody moved his head and looked at me. That doesn't sound like much, but it's a big thing for a Balloon Head to do. Of course, Bradley immediately came and questioned me after.

"What did you say to him?" Bradley demanded.

"I was asking if he'd buy me a pony for Christmas," I said.

"I know that's a joke," Bradley said, "But you better be careful what you say to them."

"What do you say to them, Bradley?"

"You don't need to know that," he told me.

He wouldn't answer any more of my questions and claimed it was for my own good that I didn't know more. If you ever get down here, maybe you could do me a favor and punch Bradley in the face? I'd do it, but I'd have to find something to stand on or maybe do it when he was lying down.

Good luck with your journey, Aaron. I'll be here waiting for you. I love you.

Joy

August 27—5:30 p.m.

Joy,

Well, I have good news and bad news. The good news is that I finally made it downtown. The bad news is, I have no idea how to find you.

You would not recognize downtown. The once tall skyscrapers are gone. Steel and glass replaced with green plants and thick, black clay. I am fairly sure I found your building, but as you said, it looks like it is mostly underground now. As are most of the buildings here. They look almost like giant snakes, with ninety percent of their bodies underground, and just their heads poking out. Like the buildings came to life and immediately burrowed beneath the earth. There is something vaguely building-like about these "heads," something I just can't put my finger on. But anyone who has never been here, and didn't know what this area looked like before, would have no idea these things had been buildings.

There are no streets anymore. The asphalt has cracked apart and shifted. So there is no way to pinpoint an exact address for sure. I'm using pure guesswork to figure out where you are, and even then it may take several tries until I get it right.

I am sitting on a bench across the street from you, as far as I can tell. Remember that little park? Well, that appears untouched. The plants may be a bit grown out and wilder, but it is essentially the same. For some reason, the laptop works here. I remember working on my laptop and drinking from a cup of Starbucks' coffee at this same exact spot in the past, when I used to come for my infrequent visits to take you to lunch. I miss the taste of real coffee. I haven't been able to find any since the tsunami. Of course, that's the least of my troubles.

I'm alone right now. Herb didn't make it. Davey attacked us yet again and took Herb away. I wasn't surprised. I knew he'd follow me and I knew that Herb's days were numbered. This time Davey told me that his food was running out and that he would have to take me next. I'm not too eager to find out if he means it. I've got the sword by my side at all times. I took a few whacks at him when he grabbed Herb, but he has such a hard outer shell that hacking away at him doesn't do much damage, and I couldn't get anywhere near his head. I have to find a better weapon.

I am sorry I wrote the comments that Davey said about you. I don't know why I did that, but now that I've reread my message, it seems cruel. I wasn't thinking. But, then again, perhaps he feels the way he does because you were the first one to notice the malevolence inside him. I was in a state of denial for much longer, and indulged him more than I should have. I just refused to believe that our child could be such a bad seed. But I don't doubt it anymore. I've seen him kill in such a cold-blooded manner, and I'm sure he would have been just as much of a predator if none of this had happened, even if he'd grown up to be a normal boy in a normal world.

Then again, there was never anything normal about him. And he actually seems content in his new monstrous identity.

There are four of the giant black beetles standing about twenty feet from where I am sitting. They aren't doing anything. They're just standing there, stone-still and silent, just like the rest of them that I've seen. I have rarely seen them in packs of four, that's a lot for them. They are facing your building, or where I think it is.

They seem to be different sizes, and I've come to think of them as The Black Beatles. Do you remember before they became famous the Beatles had been called The Silver Beatles? Well, these are the black ones. There's even a shorter one that I've come to call Ringo.

I don't think I want to go to Los Angeles anymore. I am so tired.

So now I have a question for you. I do not see any doors or windows. There are some weird frames that might have been windows at one time. And an almost mouth-like opening that looks shaped like a door. But there is no way in. No glass in the windows, no wood in the door.

138

The frames are just decorations on some featureless head of clay and grass.

I have no idea how you get oxygen in there. Or how you survive at all. You are in the belly of a whale trapped in the earth. And I have no clue how to even attempt to get inside and save you.

You've been in there awhile. Do you see any way out? Any ventilation shafts or hidden exits? All I can think to do is to dig, and I'll do that if I have to. But maybe you can make this easier for us both?

I told you I would find you. Now I have to find a way to get you out of there. And I suddenly feel unsure about whether I can do it.

There's got to be a way.

Don't give up on me.

Aaron

August 28—2:03 a.m.

Well, Aaron, I would certainly not like to give up on you. I've spent my entire life giving up. I remember being in summer day camp when I was eight, nine years old, they used to make us race around the filthy lake in Pahgrove's Public Park. Perhaps you remember it? It was the skeevy park where those homeless dudes used to nude sunbathe in the summer? OMG, that was such a huge scandal back then. If only our biggest problem now was naked filthy men with shriveled dongs and body lice … LOL!

Look at me going off the beaten path. Will I get to the point already? You always hated my storytelling abilities or lack thereof. Perhaps this lack of ability to focus is related to my tendency to give up on things?

But, let's FOCUS … I'm eight years old running on my scabby, skinny legs in disgusting Pahgrove's Public Park. Let's set the scene: Garbage strewn everyone except in the wire-mesh trash cans, rabid squirrels, killer pigeons, nude homeless men!!! Braless, busty, bleached-blonde, nineteen-year-old summer camp counselors, chain-smoking Kools, have us latchkey kids of cash-strapped parents running the length of a litter-filled, scum-topped lake on the promise that whoever gets their foot on the blue chalk line first, will get this foot-sized, white chocolate candy bar they don't make anymore and was never all that great to begin with.

I never win such things and, lord knows, I'm no athlete. But, somehow, I was in the lead and, even though the prize was a candy bar I hated, it felt great being first. I was in the homestretch … Aaron, I was going to win! Then the most popular girl, a blue-eyed honey-blonde with legs like a baby Betty Grable, yelled out:

"You're going the wrong way, Joy! Turn left! Turn left!"

And dammit, I knew I was running the right path. I saw the camp counselors in the distance getting to the butts of their Kools, nearly ready to toss their menthols at the roots of the crab apple tree, but my feet betrayed me and turned left, turned the way of defeat, into the asphalt of the nonworking sprinklers as honey-blonde Tiffany's red Keds touched the blue line of chalk and her and her confeds laughed stridently.

Yes, I quit the Girl Scouts. Yes, I dropped out of college. Yes, I never finished the widely televised-on-daytime-TV medical-billing course, though I did pay off the loan. And I wonder if Bradley fails to confide in me about the Balloon Heads because I've failed to get beyond the status of *temp* at Chen, Billings, Hall, and Hall?

So, you want me to help you locate an escape hatch? Dude, that's absolutely my calling. I've been crawling in the darkness and feeling along the sides of the walls and along the floor for a crevice, an opening, anything. And what I've found is this kind of quicksand stuff at the north end of the building. If you stick your hand in it, it almost pulls you right in. Is it a bottomless pit to nowhere? I don't know. But that's all I can tell you for now. I'll keep looking and hope you do too.

Searchingly yours,

Joy

August 30—8:18 p.m.

Joy,

I know what you must be thinking. I get so close, and then you don't hear from me. Strangely, a lot has happened since I got here. I am just outside your building, and yet I feel like I am farther away than ever.

I tried to force my way inside. Since I couldn't find any tools, I first used my hands to claw away the soil and plants to get inside, and then started using the sword. But all to no avail. Every time I think I'm making progress, the soil merely readjusts itself, almost burying me in the process, and I'm back to where I began. I have been trying to think of another way inside, but I'm not having any luck. Do you have any idea how I could get inside? Does anyone in there ever go out into the world? Do you know how they do it?

I've searched for any sign of the quicksand-type stuff you mentioned, but I haven't found anything.

While I was trying to claw my way in, something hit me from behind, knocking me sprawling into the mud. It was Davey, of course, come to taunt me again.

"I have come for you, Father," he said. "Time for you to become food."

His gargantuan body hurtled toward me. I struggled to reach the sword in time, intent on hacking him to pieces.

And then everything stopped.

It was the buzzing again, louder than ever before. And this time I knew for certain it was coming from the black beetles, the sentinels standing

143

watch over this transformed world. They seemed to all be buzzing, everywhere, in unison, and the sound was deafening, and with the sound came an almost endless series of explosions.

I thnk the time they were so patiently waiting for had finally arrived.

Davey began to erupt into a thousand volcanoes, as every growth and tumor that made up his new body exploded outward, releasing child-sized insects out into the world. Giving birth to a hundred new lives. He screamed out in agony as he was torn asunder by these things, which not only tore him apart as they clambered to get out of their eggs, but then proceeded to feed upon his plentiful flesh, a feast ready and waiting for them.

Needless to say, Davey wasn't the only one who was experiencing this. I heard other people—many of them had been hiding and I didn't even know they were there—and now they were all screaming as well, as their deformities burst open, releasing the beetles' young. Dozens of child-sized, black beasts erupting onto the earth. Every tumor, every enlarged body part, was an egg waiting to hatch. We were all just incubators for these things.

Since my foot was also enlarged, and thus yet another beetle egg, I was not spared either. My foot seemed to rupture and explode flesh and gore, the pain so severe I almost blacked out. Luckily, instead of turning on me for nourishment, the newborn creature joined its brethren in devouring Davey, who was near enough to attract it away from me.

My foot now bloody, fleshy tatters, I dragged myself away from the scene of such carnage, crawling back to the park bench where my laptop remained. But I blacked out as soon as I got close to it. The pain was just too much.

Upon awakening, I saw that my foot, or where it had been, had already healed itself, forming a hardened stump. It was as if my foot had never existed, as if I had always had just one. The pain had subsided enough for me to sit up and survey my surroundings.

Davey was no more. The insect spawn had picked him clean, leaving a hideous, elongated skeleton in its wake. A wall of bones. And there were other skeletons in the distance, sprawled on the ground, twisted into white pretzel shapes.

Somehow, I was spared.

A shadow passed me by, and I looked up to see one of the giant black beetles, I immediately believed it to be the one I called Ringo (how could I tell it was Ringo for sure? I have no idea. He looked down at me with his segmented eyes, and something passed between us. Something without words, but instead composed of a thousand images. Like I was suddenly privy to a foreign language I had never understood before. And he revealed some things to me.

The tsunami was not some alien weapon, or some hand of God, or the earth striking back at the human race that had defiled it. These creatures, which had been asleep for eons deep within the earth, had finally awakened and conjured it up to destroy our cities. Either the work of bizarre science or some kind of magic, they had used the green tsunami to crush us, and to thin out the herd so that we would be more manageable.

And those of us who survived? The green water impregnated us, man and woman alike, with these vile eggs that deformed our bodies. And the beetles were patiently awaiting the time of their hatching.

Calmly standing guard over the new millennium, when mankind would die out completely, and they would take over the surface world.

All this I saw in his red kaleidoscope eyes (and, really, I have no proof he was even male). And I knew that they had allowed me to write to you by email, that somehow they had allowed the Internet to work, and they were entertained by our conversations, as they waited and endured the passage of time.

Or at least this one creature had been entertained. And I realized how insignificant I was. How insignificant we all are, now.

I tried to lift myself up on the bench, to reason with this creature somehow. But the images passed between us in the breadth of seconds, and then it moved on, so quickly that I could not follow its progress with my eyes. And I knew it would only be a matter of time before its children needed more food and came to devour me.

As I write this now, some of the chittering creatures are nearby, as if they just realized I am here. But they are playing with me somehow, dragging my final moments out, watching me as I type this.

And now I know I will never be able to free you from your subterranean prison. And I will never see you again. And I wonder if something similar is happening where you are. And if you will survive somehow, long after I am gone.

They are advancing. My time is running out. Soon I will be like Davey.

I love y......

August 31—1:59 a.m.

Aaron,

I feel sick. Please let me know you are okay.

Love,

Joy

September 4—2:01 a.m.

Hello. It's been four days since I wrote you and still no response ... are you there, Aaron?

Can you hear my voice calling out to you from the glowing screen? Can you see these screaming words? Or is Ringo reading them? Or the Balloon Heads? Or Bradley? Or Cindy's Spanish moss? I'm going crazy. I don't think you're here anymore.

Yours Always,

Joy

September 6—2:05 a.m.

Aaron,

I know now that they read our emails.

Bradley came up to me a little while ago and asked if I'd had any more emails from you. I told him no. Bradley's mouth went crooked and he turned the color of whipped cream.

"So ...," Bradley said.

"What?"

"Do you ... do you think. They got him?"

"Who?" I asked, though of course I knew what he meant.

"The bugs. Did they get Aaron?"

When Bradley said that, it was like he punched me. He must have seen the effect it had on me, because he reached out and rubbed my arm. I started blinking like crazy because I didn't want to cry in front of Bradley.

"Joy," Bradley said, "I'm only asking because I'm thinking about our survival."

"Did you read my emails?"

"Aaron gave us some valuable information, Joy. We wanted to see if he could find a way to stop the bugs ..."

"And apparently he didn't? How disappointing for you."

I turned to leave, but Bradley grabbed my arm.

151

"Joy," he whispered, "Survival of the fittest. Haven't you figured it out?"

"I'm sorry?"

"We're underground. We're nursing the Balloon Heads. Without our care, they would die."

"No kidding," I said.

Bradley put his hands on my shoulders and looked into my eyes. "You've forgotten who you are. We ate the people on the second floor."

"We ate their fruit. We didn't eat ..." I stopped, shutting my eyes. My head was throbbing painfully.

"Them?" Bradley asked. "We ate them. There was no fruit. Cindy saw what we were really eating. There was a glitch in her veneer."

My legs were weak. I sat down on the floor.

"We aren't the Balloon Heads' captives," I said.

"We're finally getting out of here, Joy," Bradley said.

"Who is Joy?" I asked.

"You can be Joy. I don't know what to call you otherwise."

"She's dead," I said.

"For a while now," Bradley agreed.

"But I feel her. How can she not be?"

"Look," Bradley said. "It was confusing for me also. The ones that couldn't cope went to the wall."

"You're sending me to the wall?" I asked.

"You kept trying to go there. I had to stop you because we needed to learn from Aaron about the outside. Because of you, we know it's safe to come out."

"I'm Joy," I said, but I knew it was a lie.

"Your name can be Joy," Bradley said. "I still call myself Bradley."

152

"Where will Joy go without me?" I asked.

"Joy's been dead a while."

"Since the tsunami," I said. "But her consciousness?"

"It's an illusion," Bradley said. "Let it go."

"I want her here with me!" I shouted.

I stood up, Aaron, and I ran. I ran back into this room with the computer. Because that's what I do. I write to you. But you're not here anymore. And soon Joy will not be here either.

The Balloon Heads are about to pop. I can feel it. There's going to be a great feast and then we're going out into the sunlight. But I'm not hungry anymore, Aaron.

If you don't hear from me, it means I've gone to the wall.

YBWMAYW (your bug who masquerades as your wife),

Joy

September 6—2:28 a.m.

ERROR: *We were unable to deliver your message. Permanent failure.*

ABOUT THE AUTHORS

LAURA COONEY

Laura Cooney's work has appeared in various horror publications and in the anthologies *Bandersnatch* and *Dark Jesters*. *In Sickness: Stories From a Very Dark Place*, a joint short story collection she wrote in collaboration with her husband, L.L. Soares, was published by Skullvines Press in 2010. She lives in Massachusetts with her husband and their iguana, Pippi Greenstocking.

L.L. SOARES

L.L. Soares is the Bram Stoker Award-winning author of the novel *Life Rage*. His other books include the short story collection *In Sickness* (with Laura Cooney) and the novels *Rock 'n' Roll* and *Hard*. His fiction has appeared in such magazines as *Cemetery Dance*, *Horror Garage*, *Bare Bone*, *Shroud*, and *Gothic.Net*, as well as the anthologies *The Best of Horrorfind 2*, *Zippered Flesh: Tales of Body Enhancements Gone Bad!*, *Zippered Flesh 2: More Tales of Body Enhancements Gone Bad!*, *Someone Wicked: A Written Remains Anthology*, and *Traps*. He also co-writes the Stoker-nominated horror movie review column *Cinema Knife Fight*, which has a whole site built around it at cinemaknifefight.com. To keep up on his endeavors, go to www.llsoares.com.

ABOUT THE ILLUSTRATORS

JU KIM

Graduating from the Moore College of Art and Design, Ju Kim knew she wanted to pursue a career in the creative marketing world. Her favorite quote—"Things don't happen; you make them happen"—propelled her, after graduation, into a field where only 2% of each graduating class enters creative advertising/marketing. Her creative ventures have led her to work with government, nonprofit, education, and public utility clients. She currently works full-time as the Art Director for Independent School Management, where she is responsible for designing print and web graphics for ISM's many service departments, as well as assisting the Marketing Director in creative direction. Ju designed the cover for *Green Tsunami* and also created three of its illustrations.

WILL RENFRO

Will Renfro was raised by wolves in the wilds of Maine ... and likes to draw. He taught himself how to draw, never had any formal training, and has been a horror fan since the early 1970s. Back in the mid-90s, his art and story "Spaghetti Western" appeared in the comic anthology *Random Access*. In the intervening years, he has produced a good deal of work for Cemetery Dance, creating illustrations for both the magazine and comic book adaptations for *Grave Tales*. He's adapted works by William F. Nolan, Richard Laymon, Gary Raisor, Ed Gorman, and Joe Lansdale.

Will created the book cover for Novello Publishers' *Dark Jesters: An Anthology of Humorous Horror*, which was edited by Nick Cato and L.L. Soares. So, *Green Tsunami* isn't Will's first project involving L.L.!

Visit Will's website at www.renfrostudio.com.

JUSTYNN TYME

Justynn Tyme is a Buddhist, Dadaist, and multi-talented experimental artist. He is currently the Director of Radioactive Mango Recordings' ALL-OUT MONSTER REVOLT PROJECT, a member of the Written Remains Writers Guild, and steward of the Dada Network. Justynn has been a long-time fellow in many experimental arts organizations, most notably: The New Absurdist, 391, The Dada Network, and Taped Rugs Productions. Justynn's work has appeared in both national and international publications, including KBOO's *101 Hours of Innumerable Small Events*, The Written Remains Writers Guild's *Stories from the Inkslingers* and *Someone Wicked* anthologies, Full of Crow's *Corporeal Flux 2*, Mill Stream Book's *Bust Down The Door and Eat All The Chickens* and Three Room Press's premier Dada magazine "Maintenant." Justynn is the founder and director of America's most obscure Absurdist comedy group, The Whimsical Icebox; the curator of the Omphalos Dada Yow's Digital Dada Museum; and the founder of the annual, international event, Dalikrab Day. Justynn currently lives in Dada, Delaware—where he believes himself to be a ten-foot-tall eggplant from outer space—in a house of antiquity with six cats and a liquor cabinet.

DANIEL VERKYS

Dan Verkys created the wonderful cover illustration. Residing in Melbourne, Australia, Dan's work can be found in numerous publications and CD packages, both nationally and internationally. His Website (www.gardenofbadthings.com) provides an in depth look at the inner workings of his art, with updates and links to his extensive online galleries of work using the mediums of mixed media and digital compositing bringing his own perspective to the horror/fantasy genre. He has also provided his style of imagery to the film, literature and music industries.

According to Dan his ideas stem from a combination of love, fear and a distorted, overactive imagination. By day, he works in a corporate graphics environment. By night, he works on his own dark visions and on design work for a variety of entertainers, authors, and artists.

"For as long as I can remember I've had an fascination with dark imagery, in recent years my art has not been overly focused on gore or the anything too gratuitous, dark art can be so much more than that. With my work, I'm attempting to combine the sinister with the beautiful, I'm forever trying to find that balance, the point where the two meet in harmony. I'm influenced by the work of surreal artists such as Salvador Dali and Zdzislaw Beksinski, and, of course, heavily influenced by the works of H.R. Giger, among others, which for better or worse is quite evident in my work.

"The digital art realm appeals to me, I love the limitless possibilities, and the medium provides me what I need to create art that is at times thought-provoking and disturbing. There's a fine line between reality and fantasy, peace and anger, love and hate and an even finer line between sane and insane, these are all the common threads to my work, fine lines indeed, which I find myself tip toeing back and forward across in an attempt to dispel personal fears and pose possible

160

answers to some unimaginable questions. The digital world is where I create my own artistic reality where I hope people of a similar mindset can connect with."

ZIPPERED FLESH 2:
More Tales of Body Enhancements Gone Bad!

So, you loved the first **ZIPPERED FLESH** anthology? Well, here are yet more tales of body enhancements that have gone horribly wrong! Chilling tales by some of the best horror writers today, determined to keep you fearful all night (and maybe even a little skittish during the day).

Bryan Hall * Shaun Meeks * Lisa Mannetti * Carson Buckingham * Christine Morgan * Kate Monroe * Daniel I. Russell * M.L. Roos * Rick Hudson * J.M. Reinbold * E.A. Black * L.L. Soares * Doug Blakeslee * Kealan Patrick Burke * A.P. Sessler * David Benton & W.D. Gagliani * Jonathan Templar * Christian A. Larsen * Shaun Jeffrey * Jezzy Wolfe * Charles Colyott * Michael Bailey

Available in paperback and Kindle eBook from Amazon.com.
Also visit smartrhino.com for the latest from Smart Rhino Publications.

www.ingramcontent.com/pod-product-compliance
Lightning Source LLC
Chambersburg PA
CBHW070925130626

46555CB00001B/287